Life on the River

Life on the River

Written by Tom Edwards

TATE PUBLISHING & Enterprises

Published by Tate Publishing & Enterprises, LLC
127 E. Trade Center Terrace | Mustang, Oklahoma 73064 USA
1.888.361.9473 | www.tatepublishing.com

Tate Publishing is committed to excellence in the publishing industry. The company reflects the philosophy established by the founders, based on Psalm 68:11,
"The Lord gave the word and great was the company of those who published it."

Book design copyright © 2009 by Tate Publishing, LLC. All rights reserved.
Cover & interior design by Lindsay B. Behrens
Illustration by Genevieve Stotler
Backcover photo by Jamie Gould

Published in the United States of America

ISBN: 978-1-60799-452-7
1. Fiction / Short Stories   2. Fiction / General
09.07.17

In Memory of:

This book is written in loving memory of Paw and Grandpaw.

This book is dedicated to Maw, all of my brothers and sister, whose existence created these stories, and to my wife, three children and grandchildren whose being will carry me on to more "Good Old Days."

Table of Contents

Life on the River 1965

Introduction

This is a collection of short stories, born from actual events that took place on the Coosa River, which begins in the mountains of north Georgia and meanders through central Alabama, eventually merging with the Tallapoosa River. At this point, the Alabama River is formed and flows into the Gulf of Mexico.

These stories were then stretched to the max for your enjoyment and reading pleasure. Growing up on the river has left many memories that will stay with me all the way to the grave. There were five boys and one girl in our family. We didn't have a lot of money, but we had a lot of love and lots of adventures! We could all hunt, fish, and work. As I think back now, I think about those days growing up as the "Good Old Days" and remember the good times we had. Sure, there were some bad times too, but they mostly seem to be forgotten. Paw never was one to dwell on anything bad; he had rather smile and be happy. Maw was just as sweet as she could be and could work from can till can't. I don't think I have ever seen anyone with more endurance than her. To say the least, we had great parents and grandparents that helped us grow, learn and mature into responsible adults. There are many stories that could be told, but I just picked out a few to write about. I hope these stories bring a smile to your face or a tear to your eye. We all have "Good Old Days" to remember and I hope that you enjoy reading these as much as I enjoyed writing them!

River Boys

The morning fog was thick and only the dipping of a paddle could be heard on the river. A vague figure was pressing steadily along the banks of the Coosa in a flat bottom boat. The boat moved easily under the control of the navigator who plied his paddle with great expertise. Young Ken Clayburn started his day off running his trotlines, which consisted of a main line stretched across the river with staging lines tied to it every six feet. A hook tied to the staging line, bait on the hook and you are ready to catch catfish. Although he was only twelve, Ken could handle boats and knew the river as well as anyone.

Easing the boat up to the stump that his line was tied to, Ken ran the paddle down and retrieved it. There was always a look of excitement and anticipation in his eyes when he first touched the line. Ken pulled his boat along going from hook to hook, baiting the empty hooks with crawfish, stumpknockers, chub minnows and other small fish that he had seined up in his net the day before. Suddenly the line started moving up current slowly and steady. Ken broke a smile because he knew he had a big catfish. Only the large fish pull steady and strong, while a smaller one jerks sharply and quickly.

As he got closer, bubbles came up and swirls of water boiled to the top. A giant tail came out of the water. "He's got to weigh thirty pounds," Ken said to himself. Just then the big cat figured out that something had a hold of him and made a hard dive. Ken was expecting this, but caught up in excitement, wasn't ready. It was a powerful dive, sliding the line through his hands and sinking one of the hooks into his palm. Grasping the main line tightly to loosen the pressure on the hook, Ken shouted out a strong word he had learned on the numerous fishing trips taken with his grandpaw.

The fish quit diving and slack came into the line. Ken quickly took his knife and cut the staging line that the hook was tied to. He grabbed the extra paddle, tied it to the line and said, "Pull on that awhile," as he released it.

The hook was in past the barb and Ken knew what he had to do. Either pull it out backwards with the barb pulling a big hunk of flesh out with it or push it through. The hook was sharp, so Ken decided to push it through his skin. Gritting his teeth, he pulled on the hook and the point pushed the skin up as the tip of the hook barley broke through. *That's not going to work,* he thought as he breathed deeply, trying to keep from passing out. His face was turning white as the blood left his head. *Just snatch it!* He thought as he wrapped the staging line around his other hand and gave a quick jerk. Profanity rang out across the river again. The hook was all the way through now. The hard part done, Ken took his pliers and cut the eye of the hook off. The hook slid out easily and some color came back to his face as he tied his handkerchief around his hand to stop the bleeding.

Boy that was stupid, he thought. His Grandpaw and Paw had told him many times not to let the line slide through his hands when there was a big fish on.

Meanwhile the paddle had been bobbing up and down all this time wearing the big cat down. Then , Ken eased up to the paddle and grabbed the line tight, knowing that he wouldn't let that happen again. Slowly pulling the boat along the line to the hook that the tired catfish was on, he dipped him up without a battle. It was a big fish for the boy, but he lifted it into the boat easily.

Ken was tall and lean, but there was power in his muscles from hard work. There wasn't much money around and the Clayburns grew crops, livestock, and lived off the land. There's no room for being lazy, living like this and no excuses for not getting the job done.

Paddling back home, Ken enjoyed the summer morning. Everything was still and quiet on the river. He had a feeling for the river that ran deep in his soul. Love for the life and enjoyment of the river and respect for the dangers sometimes there. This was passed down to him from his Grandpaw and Paw, who he listened to with much respect.

Pulling up to the dock at home, Ken was tying up the boat when his younger brother, Will, came running. Will always loved to meet Ken when he came in off the river to see what he had caught. "Hey Ken, did you get anything?" asked Will.

"Just a little ole cat," Ken said, not letting Will see that he was excited. He felt this made him look bigger.

"Gol–lee, what a fish! Paw, Paw, come look what Ken caught!" Will clamored.

Paw walked down to the boat and said, "That's a nice blue cat you got there. Better tie him out in the creek for a couple of weeks to let some of the fat burn off. Then we'll have us some bluecat steaks," and walked back to what he was doing with a big grin on his face. Paw was always proud of us when we made a big catch and knew what he was talking about too. Big catfish have layers of fat on the meat that taste real bad. By tying them out in a clean creek, he wouldn't eat and some of the fat would burn off.

Ken and Will tied a good rope to the fish's jaw and carried it to the creek. While tying him to a stump at the edge of the creek, Grandpaw walked up. "Hey boys, that's a real nice fish you got there. It must weigh about thirty–five pounds."

"He sure put up a fight," Ken said, trying to hide his hand behind his back, not wanting his Grandpaw to know what had happened.

"A big cat like that could hurt a boy if he didn't hold that line tight," said Grandpaw.

"Yes sir," said Ken, not feeling so sure about himself now. Will was still staring at the fish with wide eyes, not knowing what had happened or saying anything.

"Well, I've got some plowing to do," Grandpaw said, turning to go. He turned back slowly, asking, "Did you see anyone else out on the river this morning?"

Ken said, "No sir, just me and the fog."

"That's strange," said Grandpaw. "I could have sworn that I heard someone hollering. I hope nothing went wrong with anybody out there."

Grandpaw went on about his business and Ken was thinking, *He knows it was me and he knows what I said. He just wants me to sweat awhile.* Ken turned around and Will was still standing in the same place, staring at the catfish. "You're going to stare a hole in that fish if you don't quit looking at him," said Ken. "Come on, let's go catch some bait and I'll let you help me bait the lines this evening." That snapped Will out of his trance.

"Oh boy, can I really? Let's go!" Will said with lights dancing in his eyes.

Ken loved his little brother and always tried to teach him something about river life. At the time he didn't know it, but these lessons turned out to be most important in not only river life, but life in general. Ken was just passing on what he had learned.

"Ken, are we going down to the spring to catch some crawfish?" Will asked.

"No," replied Ken.

"Ken, are we going to the barn and dig some worms?"

"No," replied Ken.

"Ken, are we going to check the wire baskets?"

"No," replied Ken.

"Ken, are we going to catch some bait and go fishing?"

"Yes," Ken replied.

"Ken, where are we going to catch bait at?"

"In the pond," he replied.

"Ken, what kind of bait are we going to catch?"

"Big bait," Ken replied.

"Why?" Will asked.

"Will, you ask too many questions," Ken said. "Just be patient and you will find out."

Patience wasn't one of little Will's best quali-ties, but he was getting a lesson on his way to catch bait. It didn't seem like much of a lesson then, but was a step in his education that could and probably would save his life one day. Ken glanced at Will and grinned. He was doing the same thing for Will that had been done for him. Life lessons will always continue as long as someone is open enough to receive them from others.

Will was quiet now, with maybe a little fear showing in his eyes. His young mind had about figured out how they were going to catch bait and it wasn't something that he liked to do. "Ken, we're not going to seine are we?"

"Yep," Ken replied. "I want to catch some big bait. Big bait catches big fish."

"Can't we just catch them with a cane pole?" Will asked.

"Well, we could, but the big seine will be faster," Ken replied.

Ken knew that Will was afraid of seining bait. They had seined one time before and a six pound carp had jumped out of the water and smacked Will right in the face. It had almost knocked him out and Ken had to go to his rescue before he drowned. Now Ken wasn't antagonizing his little brother. His Paw had taught him that to overcome fear, you have to face it. Ken was trying to help Will overcome that fear.

Ken got the seine out of the shed and started unrolling it. In the meantime, Will was getting a little fidgety. Ken asked Will, "Do you want the deep end or the shallow end?"

"I don't want either end. I can run and get Paw to help you and then I can carry the bait bucket, okay?" Will was trying to get out of the situation.

"Well, I guess you could, but then Paw would be the one going fishing with me." Ken was pressuring Will to face his fear and he knew that his little brother had it in him. He just needed a little help.

"You said I could go with you!" said Will.

"Yes, I did," said Ken. "But you have to help me catch the bait." Ken could see the wheels turning in Will's head. He was trying to think of a way out. Then his expression changed. He was going to face his fear. "Okay, I'll do it, but I want the shallow side. Those big carp are out in deep water," said Will with a little satisfaction.

"Good," said Ken. "I was hoping that you would say that. Those big carp don't bother me at all. It's those snakes on the shallow end that scare me."

"No, they don't," said Will. "You're just trying to scare me."

With the joking aside, Ken and Will started seining around the edge of the pond. Will was doing a fine job, too. "Hold it up," said Ken. "I'll circle around now and we'll drag it up on the bank." As Ken circled around to hem the bait up, fish started jumping everywhere.

"Look at all those fish!" Will exclaimed.

"Yeah, we got them this time," said Ken. The boys pulled the seine up on the bank and it wasn't easy. There was enough bait to fish a whole year with in that seine.

"Run get the bucket," said Ken excitedly. Will was just standing there smiling. He'd never seen so many fish in a seine. "Go get the bucket, Will. They won't live forever out of the water," said Ken again. Will came back with the bucket and started scooping bait. "Hold on Will. We don't need them all. We'll just pick out some big ones and turn the rest loose," said Ken.

"Turn them loose? We can't turn them loose," stammered Will.

"Yes, we can," said Ken. "Then the next time we need bait, we'll know where to come."

They loaded the bucket up with the biggest ones and quickly turned the others loose. Will, having a big ole time, picked up the bucket and started to the boat landing. It was so heavy that he could only take a few steps at a time and then he would have to set it down. Ken was admiring his little brother and let him go for awhile. Seeing that Will was getting tired, Ken asked, "Want me to carry the bucket awhile?"

"No," Will spurted out quickly. "I can carry it myself." Will had really stepped up and Ken was proud of him, but he knew that it would be dark before they got to the boat.

"I know you can, but it would be easier if we both carried it together, like Paw used to help me do when we had a real heavy load."

Will set the bucket down, but he wasn't giving up. You could see the determination in his face. "Okay, we'll carry it together."

The boys made it to the landing and loaded up the boat with everything they needed. "We'll go up river first and work our way back down," said Ken. Off they went with Will proudly paddling to whatever lay ahead.

Ken had told Will to save the biggest bait for last, and when they had finished baiting all the trot lines, Will reminded him.

"Ken, you didn't use this big bream. You kept telling me to save it," said Will, very concerned about the last bait.

"Oh," said Ken. "I almost forgot. Hand me that jug right there." There was a one gallon plastic jug lying in the bottom of the boat. Ken opened a box and pulled out the biggest hook Will had ever seen.

"Gol–lee, we could catch a whale on that," Will said.

"Maybe, but we're just after a big catfish," said Ken, as he tied a four foot piece of heavy line to the jug, an old spark plug for a sinker and then the big hook.

"Hand me that big bream," Ken said. Will handed him the bait and Ken hooked it up and handed it to Will. "Here, you throw it out. Maybe you will bring us good luck."

Will took the jug line and looked around as if he was making sure that this was a good place to throw it out. "This looks like a good place."

"Yep, I think you're right," said Ken, with a smile.

Will talked up a storm all the way home about how many big cats they would catch tomorrow. All through supper he talked about how many big cats they would catch tomorrow. Then Will went to bed talking about how many big cats they would catch tomorrow.

After Will had gone to bed, Paw told Ken, "You be careful with Will out there tomorrow. You may have to make two or three trips to unload all those big catfish if ya'll catch as many as Will said you would." They both laughed and went to bed.

"Ken, wake up, wake up!" said Will as he shook his older brother.

"What time is it?" Ken asked sleepily.

"It's time to go check the trotlines!" said Will with great excitement.

Ken got out of bed and got dressed. They loaded up the boat and had to wait thirty minutes for daylight. Will had gotten a jump start on this morning. After running both trotlines and only catching four fair size cats, Will was looking disappointed. Ken was a little bewildered himself. "We should have loaded the boat," Ken said. "I don't know why we didn't."

"We've still got the jug with that big bream on it," said Will with his last glimmer of hope.

"That's right, we do," said Ken. "Let's go find it."

The boys looked and looked for the jug, but it was nowhere to be found. After two hours of paddling around looking for it, they were back to the spot where Will had thrown it out. "I guess we're out of luck today," said Ken, looking at a very disappointed little brother. Will didn't even make a comment. He was so disappointed. "We might as well head back," said Ken. The boys picked up their paddles and slowly headed home.

About the time they started paddling, low and behold, the jug popped up out of the water right beside the boat. "There it is!" hollered Will.

"I see it!" hollered Ken. "Grab it!" Will made a grab for the jug, but it took off. "Paddle fast!" said Ken. They chased that jug all over the place. Every time they got close to it, under it went and they waited for it to come back up.

"We got a whale on there!" Will exclaimed.

"It might be. I never saw one run this far and long before," said Ken.

The pace finally slowed down and none too soon. The boys were worn out from paddling and the big catfish or whatever it was, was worn down, too.

"When we get up beside it, I'll grab the jug and you get the net ready," said Ken.

"Okay," said Will.

They paddled up to the jug and it didn't even move. Ken was thinking to himself, *I hope it didn't get off.* He grabbed the jug and it hadn't gotten off.

The bluecat was so big that it frightened the boys as it slashed its mighty tail, soaking them with water. It seemed as though the fish was playing a game with them. Probably thinking that such small fishermen couldn't possibly land him and a smirk seemed to be on his face as he thrashed his tail again. "Net him!" Ken hollered. Will was trying to, but the fish wouldn't go into the net.

"The net's not big enough. It's too big for the net!" hollered Will. It's a good thing that catfish was about worn out.

The bluecat had made one big mistake. He had underestimated his young adversaries, thinking that he could play his game and overpower them in the end. Ken held strong as the fish made his powerful dives. At one point, Will had to grab hold of Ken's legs to keep him from being pulled out of the boat. The fish had put up a mighty battle, but couldn't outlast the sheer determination of the young fishermen.

Slowly, his dives weakened and he floated belly up. The smirk that had been on his face earlier: now replaced with the face of defeat. Ken pulled it up beside the boat and Will got a rope around his head. "We'll have to drag him home. I don't think we can get him in the boat," said Ken.

They tied another rope around the big fish, sat back and rested as they looked at him. "I didn't know that there were fish that big in this river," said Will in a state of disbelief.

"I didn't either. I never would have landed him without your help," said Ken and smiled at his brother.

The boys were tired, but showed no sign of their exhaustion; they were far too excited about their massive catch. They laughed and talked as they paddled all the way home. When they got home, Paw and Grandpaw were standing on the bank waiting on them and they didn't look happy. "Oh no, we're in trouble," said Will in a concerned voice.

"Not for long, once they see this fish," Ken whispered.

They paddled the boat right up beside Paw, who was standing there with his hands on his hips. "You better have a good story for this one. It's three o'clock in the afternoon," said Paw looking sternly at Ken.

"It's my fault," claimed Will. "I...we caught the biggest fish in the whole river." Will was hanging in there. Surprised by young Will's acceptance of responsibility, there was a twinkle in Paw's eyes.

"Well, where is this biggest fish in the whole river?" Paw asked having a hard time not smiling.

Ken pulled on the rope and the big catfish slid up to the bank. He had never seen Paw or Grandpaw speechless, with their mouths wide open, but they were now. "There he is," Will proudly proclaimed, "A Coosa River whale cat." With that everyone laughed.

Ken and Will had caught the biggest fish ever heard of on the Coosa River—one hundred twenty– four pounds; Ken and Will were on cloud nine.

After all the excitement, the boys finally collapsed in their beds, both dreaming about the monster catfish that they had caught. Paw let them sleep late, knowing how tired the boys were. Ken was dreaming that he was running a trotline and a fish was tugging on it. Then he woke up and it was Will tugging on his pajama shirt. "Wake up Ken, wake up," Will said hurriedly.

"What you in such a hurry for?" Ken asked groggily.

"We got to catch some bait and it won't wait," said Will happily. "We got a pond to seine."

"I thought you didn't like seining," said Ken.

"I didn't, but now I do," boasted Will.

"Well, what if one of those carp jumps up and hits you right in the mouth?" asked Ken with a smile.

Will thought for a minute and replied, "Well, I guess a boy that catches a one hundred twenty–four pound catfish can't be afraid of a little six pound carp. I guess I'll give it a kiss and keep on seining." Will was full of himself now. He even walked different, kinda older like.

As Ken and Will headed for the pond to seine some bait, Grandpaw and Paw sat on the porch watching the boys. Paw chuckled and said, "There go a couple of fishermen."

Grandpaw spit a stream of tobacco and said, "Yep, there go two river boys. Yes sir, reminds me of you when you were that age. River men in the making."

The moral of this story is ...
Determination and will power can and
will help you achieve your objectives in life.

What's That in The Sky?

November 15, 1973 was a fine day and Big John and I decided we'd go hunting on the other side of the river. John got his nickname "Big John" when he was born. He weighed fifteen pounds and four ounces. In the first grade he weighed 120 lbs and now, at the age of fourteen, he tops the scales at 275 lbs and is 6'8" tall.

Big John's right handy to have around for a little brother. I can hide behind him if our bull catches us out in the pasture. When we go coon hunting, instead of bear hugging the tree, John just picks me up and sets me on the first limb. When we're fishing and catch so many fish that the back of the boat starts sinking, I just move John to the front to even things out. Just don't put him in a canoe. I did this one time and that was the last time. I was in the back of the canoe and eased up to the dock. I told John to gently step down into the canoe. Well, he just baled off in it and shot me like a catapult over the dock and up into the woods. I rolled right into a big patch of poison oak and that stuff tore me up. It was about a month before I got rid of that rash. So, no more canoe rides for John.

We loaded up the boat with our shotguns, ten cans of viennas, ten cans of sardines, two boxes of crackers, and our one–of–a–kind hunting dog, Rattler. Rattler got his name when he was about six months old. We just called him puppy until one day when I was walking through the woods and he was just ahead of me. I thought he was just playing like he was hunting, but it was the real thing. The hair on his back bristled up and I heard that snake start rattling. This was a big snake; he could strike a distance of two and a half feet and was about five feet long. When he struck, puppy jumped sideways and dodged those deadly fangs. Then he grabbed that snake behind the head, breaking its neck. I'd never seen anything like it in my life. Puppy became Rattler right there and was the most famous dog on the Coosa River.

Rattler was a Jack Russell—eighteen pounds of twisted blue steel. He could tree a coon and whip a coon, hunt opossums, squirrels, rabbits, deer, beaver, muskrat and retrieve fish I had shot with my bow. I'm telling you, Rattler is a very special dog.

We crossed the river and tied the boat in the back of Sulfur Branch. Rattler jumped out and was running back and forth, ready to start hunting, but he didn't know what we wanted to hunt. I told John to start kicking around in the grass and he did. Rattler immediately knew we were going rabbit hunting. It took him about five minutes and he was running a big swamp rabbit around in a circle, bringing him back to us.

By sunset we had our limit of rabbits and were ready to head home. Big John said "Maw sure will be proud of us for bringing supper home."

"She sure will John, but you know Maw and Paw are always proud of us," I told him. We laughed, loaded up the boat and started back across the river.

Unknown to us, we were being watched by some type of mysterious aircraft. We had never seen or heard of anything like this, but we were in danger and would soon find out.

About halfway across, Big John looked up and asked, "What's that in the sky?" I looked up and saw something like I'd never seen before. It was a big 'ole light like a full moon, but it was moving and coming right over us. I shut off the motor and watched this thing come over us. It didn't make any noise, but it was huge and Big John was feeling uneasy. "What's that in the sky, Bill?"

"I don't know," I told him. "I've never seen anything like it and if it keeps coming, we're out of here."

Well, it kept coming and everything got real light. I decided we'd better get and tried to crank the motor, but it wouldn't start. By then Rattler was barking like crazy and it was right over us. The next thing I knew, a beam of light came down and started pulling Rattler up in the air. I wasn't about to let it take Rattler, so I grabbed him and it started pulling me, too. "Big John, hold us down. It ain't taking Rattler!" I said. Big John wrapped his big paws around my ankles and I felt that we were safe, but then it started picking Big John up, too.

Up we went into the light. We couldn't see what was up there because the light was so bright. I knew it had to be something mighty powerful to pick up Big John, but I wasn't letting go of Rattler and Big John wasn't letting go of me. That's the way we were raised and if one of us let our brother down in a time of need; we had to answer to Paw.

We lost consciousness sometime and awoke lying on a metal floor. I still had hold of Rattler and John still had a hold on me. I tried to get up but couldn't. John had me so tight that I couldn't move my legs. "John, let me go!" I hollered.

John let go and asked, "Where are we Bill?"

"I don't know, but this sure don't look like the Pearly Gates!" I exclaimed. There was shiny metal everywhere. At first I thought that we were in one of those fancy kitchens like we see on those cooking shows, but there wasn't no chef, so I discarded that idea. There were bright lights that seemed to come from nowhere, no light fixtures, just light. The light reflecting of off the spotless metal hurt our eyes and we squinted in discomfort, but at least we were alive.

"We must be in a space ship," I told John. About that time a door slid open just like on Star Trek. Rattler's hair bristled up and he started growling. I was expecting a skinny green man with a big head and no ears, but I was wrong.

Three of the most beautiful women that I'd ever seen came through the door.

They wore short dresses that appeared to be made from aluminum foil and they didn't use the whole roll. Their rosy cheeks reflected the color of their bright red, mid length hair and light green eyes gazed into ours. Long slim legs supported by what I would say is a new definition of high heels, gave them the appearance of New York models about to walk down the runway. The pleasant looks on their faces eliminated any feelings of danger; just amazement remained.

We were standing there with our mouths wide open, staring at those good looking things when John asked, "Bill, are we in heaven?"

"We might be," I told him, "And they look like they could be angels."

I figured that I might try to communicate with them. "Greetings, my name is Bill, that's John and that's my dog Rattler," I said. They just stood there looking pretty. So I decided to offer them my hand in friendship. I took a step forward and stuck out my hand. In return, I was zapped by some kind of electrical shock and it sent me to my knees. John and Rattler jumped forward to help and they got zapped, too. Then everything went black and I could see those girls smiling as I went out.

We woke up sometime later, strapped in chairs with wires attached all over us. I was in a regular chair, John was in two chairs tied together and Rattler was on a booster seat strapped to a chair with his paws sticking straight out, sitting on his butt just like us. They must not have known that Rattler was a dog. "Maw's gonna be mad cause we didn't come home," said Big John.

"And Paw's gonna tan my hide for getting us into this awful mess," I said.

We were kept captive there for hours with those wires hooked to us, probing into our bodies and brains. I had to get us out of this jam. I said, "John, we got to get Rattler to chew these straps in two, but we got to show him what to do." I tried to rock my chair over, but it was fastened tight. "John, try to rock your chair loose. If you can fall over against me and start chewing these straps, Rattler will know what to do," I said.

"I'll try," John said.

John rocked over in a flash. I don't think they knew how much it took to hold him down. He started chewing on my straps and Rattler caught on real quick. It took about thirty seconds for

Rattler to chew through his straps. One minute later we were all free and pulling wire off.

"It's time to get out of here," I said, but there was no place to go. We didn't even know whether we were in outer space or still hovering over the Coosa River. About that time, a door opened and in came the alien women. They were smiling at us and I don't know why because we had just escaped. We were standing there not knowing what to do when one of them spoke.

"I'm sorry we had to put you through this. My name is Venus and these are my sisters Rita and Vita. We are from planet Oray." *Well, this is a better greeting,* I thought.

Venus said, "We are here studying life on your planet. We have studied your people all around your world." Now I was thinking this must be a good thing because they're not mad at us for escaping.

I said, "Well, ladies, what did you think of us? I know we're just old country boys."

Venus said, "We are amazed by your ability and good looks. You are the first ones to break free from the monitor chairs. Your intelligence level is far superior to all our other specimens."

John asked, "What does that mean, Bill?" and I told him that it was good and he just smiled.

Seeing this as a good opportunity, I said, "Ladies, if you really want to examine our life-styles, we're having a dance Saturday night and all three of ya'll can come as my date. All you've got to do is put us back in our boat and we'll pick you up Saturday at five o'clock."

"We intend to replace you in your vessel, but we're going to keep your pet," Venus said.

That struck me the wrong way. There was no way I was going to leave Rattler on this spaceship. I said "Sorry, ladies, but there's no way you're going to keep Rattler. He's the best friend a man can have; he's the best hunting dog around; he's better than all those European hounds. Why, he's the best dog south of the North Pole and he stays with us." They were looking kinda confused. I don't think that they had ever had a man talk to them like this.

"We must keep your Rattler to take back to our planet to show them a product of your life-style," Venus said.

"I'll give you something to carry back," I said. "I'll bet you never had a Coosa River kiss from a Coosa River man."

Venus asked, "What is this that you are talking about? I do not understand."

"Yep, that's what I figured," I said "Let me demonstrate, but don't shock me again because this won't hurt a bit."

The girls walked back a few steps and discussed this demonstration and then walked right up to me. Venus, who must have been the chief alien said, "We will let you demonstrate this Coosa River Kiss and if it is a good enough example of human behavior, we will let you keep your dog."

This will be a piece of cake. I thought, with a big smile on my face.

Then Rita said, "If it is not a worthy example to carry back to our planet, we will carry you." This put a little more pressure on me, but I had rather have them take me than to take Rattler.

Then Vita added, "And your dog." With a smile that really had me sweating, but there was no backing out now. Once again, my mouth had gotten us into a jam and my lips were the only thing that could get us out.

Some type of video camera came out of the wall and I asked them what it was for. Venus said, "We must record this demonstration for our study of your people. You may proceed now."

I didn't hold anything back. I gave Venus all I had and then the same for Rita and Vita. Their feet slowly rose off the floor, as though the kiss was levitating them.

Venus looked at her sisters and they gave a dazed nod of their heads. Then Venus turned to me with her green eyes twinkling like stars and a most satisfied look on her face, "That was a very good demonstration. It will be sufficient."

"Okay, Ladies, now that you know what a Coosa River Kiss is, you can put this Coosa River Man and his buddies back in our Coosa River boat."

I was kinda demanding and John said, "You told them Bill." It was a bluff of course, but I figured that they were still stunned from my savage kisses (that sounds good) and would do just what I told them to. It worked. The next thing I knew, we were back in that beam of light and into our boat.

John said, "Wow, that's the most exciting thing that I've ever done! Will we ever see them again, Bill?"

"Sure we will," I told John. "I ain't never laid a kiss like that on a girl and her not come back. We'll probably see them Saturday night. Now, let's get these rabbits back home in time for supper."

"Oooooeeee!" said John. "Let's go!"

I was giving Venus another sample kiss, which we were both enjoying when I was jolted back into reality by Maw shaking me awake. As I woke, my lips were tingling and I had a big smile on my face.

"Wake up Bill. What are you smiling about?"

My smile disappeared as I realized where I was at. I sat up in bed looking around for those space girls, but saw nothing but the walls of my bedroom and Maw standing there with her hands on her hips, wondering what was wrong with me.

"Bill, why did you go to bed with all your clothes on? You didn't even take off your shoes. Wash up now and come to the table, we're having rabbit for supper."

I was having a hard time understanding what was going on; one minute I was kissing a beautiful alien girl in a space ship and the next thing I knew, I was back home. I must have been dreaming, but it seemed so real. I touched my lips with my hand and could still feel a slight tingling sensation.

Days turned to weeks and then to months as I found myself sitting outside at night watching the skies for some sign that there was alien life out there somewhere. Big John had no recollection of the abduction and thought that I had lost my mind when I had questioned him about it.

One night as Rattler and I sat outside gazing at the stars, I noticed a strange light coming out of the east. I didn't get very excited about it at first, knowing that it was probably just another airplane. As it passed by, Rattler stood up and began to growl. For a moment, I thought, *maybe…naw.* and lay back on the ground with my hands behind my head as Rattler continued to growl.

"There ain't anything out there." I told Rattler, closing my eyes and picturing the three girls lining up for another Coosa River Kiss. Instantly, my lips began to tingle. I was back in the space ship, my arms wrapped around Venus, kissing her passionately and then I opened my eyes to see Rattler licking me in the mouth.

The Moral of this story is ...
Everything you see lends to the imagination
and the imagination to the soul.

The Trail

The trail was dim and had been bypassed by everyone for many years. Today for some reason, it is caught by someone's eye. The eye of an experienced woodsman who knew all these woods and had never seen this trail before. A close examination revealed that it had been covered over by soil and leaves, perhaps the reason nobody had ever noticed it, but today it stood out, for whatever reason.

The young woodsman bent down and scraped the soil and leaves off the trail. This revealed a deep path that had been packed hard over many years, so hard that it was almost like clay pavement. *How long would it take to pack a trail this hard?* He wondered to himself. Uncovering more of the trail showed it to be wide as well. The path had clearly been traveled by many people, many times.

Now his curiosity was up. *I wonder where this trail went and who traveled it? It must have been an Indian trail, but where would it go to? A trail like this must have gone to a large village.* Clearing off more of the trail, the young man stood on it. Standing there, barefooted, on the hard packed clay, the hair on his arms started to rise and a chill surrounded him. It was almost like someone was standing beside him. The feeling was so real that he turned and looked for someone, but no one was there.

He stepped off the trail, trying to understand what was happening. The chill went away and the hair on his arms lay down. *This is kind of spooky,* he thought as he continued to look around. Stepping back on the trail, the chill returned and a fog rolled in around him. "That's enough," he said and jumped back off of the trail. Searching around him, he decided to leave. It was starting to get dark and, he reasoned, he could always return tomorrow.

On his way home he continued to look around him. This had really spooked him and he didn't scare easily. "I'll ask old J.W. about that trail. He's been around here for almost a hundred years. If anyone knows anything about this trail, he will," he said to himself trying to reason things out.

He stopped by J.W.'s house right at dark. J. W. was an old woodsman, maybe in his late eighties, who had hunted, trapped, logged and farmed this part of the country all of his life. He had more knowledge of the history and lay of the land than anyone. J. W. was smart, well respected and still in good physical condition for his age and was tough as nails.

Making a short detour, Bart stopped by J. W.'s old weathered gray house that was built by J. W. and his father, out of the trees on their land. It had never been painted, but was still very solid, being built out of heart pine.

Bart arrived at J. W.'s house in the dimming light of nightfall. When he stepped up on the porch to knock on the door, something slammed into the wall, scaring him half to death. "What's wrong boy, you a little jumpy ain't you?" J. W. laughed. J.W. liked the young man and it made his day to catch him off guard. He just couldn't resist slamming the dishpan against the wall.

"J.W., you like to have made me jump out of my britches," he said.

"Not you, not Bart Mason the great mountain man. Born a hundred years later than his time. Admired and respected by all the men because of your uncanny woodsmanship and courage in all situations. Not you, not Bart Mason that makes women swoon, just by your mere presence!" said J.W. laughing his head off.

"All right, all right, that's enough. You got me good. No need in riding me in the ground about it," Bart said with a hint of irritation in his voice.

After J.W. stopped laughing, he asked, "Well, what's got you so jumpy boy?"

"I found an old trail today down at the lower end of Brandy Holler," said Bart.

"Probably a deer trail," J.W. responded.

"No this ain't no deer trail. It's two feet wide and six inches deep and packed hard like smooth pavement," said Bart.

"I know just about every tree in that holler and I ain't never seen a trail like that. A trail like that would stick out like a sore thumb," said J.W.

"I thought I knew those woods pretty good myself," said Bart. "But the trail is there and there's something real strange about it. I had a feeling there was someone there watching me the whole time."

"Sounds to me like you got the jitters. A man's imagination can make all kinds of things happen when he gets spooked," said J.W.

"It wasn't my imagination. It's there and I keep wondering where it leads to and who traveled on it. A trail like that must have taken a long time to pack down like that or there were just a lot of people using it. It must have been an Indian trail. There had to have been a large village close by," said Bart.

J.W. was rubbing his beard and scratching his chin. "You know, I seem to remember back when I was just a kid, my granddaddy talking about Indian spirits in Brandy Holler. He actually told us kids not to be messing around down there, but I've been through those woods many a time and never noticed anything out of the normal."

"Well, I'm going back down there tomorrow and see if I can figure out where that trail leads to," Bart said with strong intention.

"Watch yourself!" J.W. spurted. "Those spirits might carry you off to the happy hunting grounds!" And he started laughing again.

That was about all Bart could take for one night. He stepped off J.W.'s porch and headed home. J.W. was still laughing in the distance, but Bart wasn't paying attention to that. He was thinking about the trail and where it could lead to. He had always been able to figure things out, but this one had him baffled. Indian spirits, getting chilled and the fog that mysteriously appeared. It was a long time before he fell asleep that night.

The next morning, he awoke after a night full of dreams and his mind was really running wild now. He'd had two dreams last night. One started on the trail. There was a fog in the air and the trail was there in front of him. He followed it for a long time, but never got anywhere, always ending up at the foot of the same hill. In the other dream, there was a trail going in both directions, but he didn't know which way to go. He heard an eagle call and looked as the eagle flew over the hill along the trail. Then he heard a painful wailing in the other direction.

Turning to look, there were buzzards circling over the trail and the wailing coming from beyond. As he watched, the buzzards got lower and lower to the ground and the wailing stopped. The eagle called again and when he turned to look, there were two eagles. They were carrying a long snake. One had the tail and the other the head, stretched out between them. They flew over his head and down to where the buzzards had been.

The eagles released the snake and there was an awful sound as it reached the ground. It was the sound of war. Gun shots, clashing metal and screams and then the snake came down the trail toward him, its mouth open wide, huge fangs dripping with blood. It was coming fast, but he couldn't move. He was trying to get out of the way, but his muscles just wouldn't work. The snake was upon him and death was with it. It opened its great jaws to strike its victim and Bart awoke from his dream. Cold and sweaty, short of breath and heart racing, *that was almost too real,* he thought.

After the dreams, Bart wasn't sure whether he should even go anywhere near the trail again. The first dream had him going around in circles and never getting anywhere. The second dream had him powerless and looking death straight in the eyes. "Just a bunch of hogwash. They don't mean anything," he said, trying to reassure himself. "I'll go check it out and put an end to these dreams."

Bart headed for Brandy Holler by way of J.W.'s house. When he got to J.W.'s, nobody was home. J.W. was always home since he had gotten older and couldn't get around as well as he used to. The day was starting off strange and he hadn't even gotten to Brandy Holler.

Bart took his time as he approached the trail. It was almost like he was sneaking up on it. He was a little uneasy for sure. "It's still here," he said to himself as if he thought it might not be. Easing up to the trail, he observed everything like he was walking through a pit full of snakes. The trail looked different; someone had uncovered more of it. Slowly stepping onto the trail, all his senses alert, Bart could see the trail more clearly. A smooth paved path leading to who knows where. As he walked forward he could see the path clearly going up and over the hill. There was no chill, no uneasy feeling, just an old trail.

Feeling better about it now, he walked on at a faster pace, wanting to know where the trail went and what was at the end. He walked awhile and stopped, but it didn't seem that he was any closer to the top of the hill. He started running faster and faster, but still he couldn't reach the top of the hill. Bart stopped, out of breath from running, *What's going on now? I'm not getting anywhere.*

About that time, he heard an eagle call. Looking up the hill he could see the eagle gliding above the trail. Bart quickly looked around behind him, remembering the dream from last night. No sign of the snake. He turned and started back up the hill toward the eagle, still calling and gliding above the trail. This time he was actually gaining ground, closer to the top now, almost there. He turned and looked one more time behind him and then topped the hill. Standing there in amazement, blinking and rubbing his eyes, Bart looked out upon a great Indian village. A beautiful valley along the river with men, women, children and dogs going about their everyday activities.

A young Indian man was carrying four fish up from the river and an Indian woman was working on a deer hide that was stretched out on the ground in front of her wigwam, which was framed out of sticks and poles and covered with animal hides. Children were playing and dogs barking at them as they ran through the village.

"This can't be," he said to himself. The eagle was floating in the air above the village. It was beautiful, like time had stood still for three hundred years. Then another eagle appeared and was desperately calling and both eagles flew off together. *I must still be dreaming,* Bart thought. Then there were gun shots and screaming; a band of Spanish soldiers wearing metal helmets and breast plates were attacking the village. The Indians fought back, but to little avail. The Spanish were cutting them down with muskets and swords, even the women and children were being butchered.

The woman that had been working on the deer hide, screamed for her children and ran to them. The young fisherman fought bravely to save his people until a musket ball ended his life.

Setting fire to the wigwams, the soldiers spared no one.

Bart wanted to help, but couldn't move. Just like in his dream, he was helpless. Then he saw J.W., dressed in buckskin and coonskin cap with an old muzzleloader rifle. He was shooting the soldiers, trying to help the Indians, but was outnumbered and had to run. There were Indians running in all directions trying to escape the soldiers and J.W. was running straight toward Bart on the trail. "Run boy!" J.W. hollered as he ran with four Spanish soldiers right behind him with swords drawn. One of them was very fast and caught up with J.W., swinging his sword and nearly cutting J.W.'s arm off. J.W. turned and fired his last shot into the soldier, dropped his rifle, and came running, holding his dangling arm with his good arm. "Run boy, before its too late!" he hollered again as he ran past Bart. But Bart couldn't move. His muscles were frozen stiff. The other three soldiers were coming fast. Bart could see their faces and eyes and their deadly intentions grimaced on their faces, blood dripping off of their swords, blood of the Indians that they had just killed. Closer now, they were upon him with bloody swords swinging toward his head. He knew his time was up as the sword closed in on his neck.

Bart jumped straight up in the bed, throwing covers everywhere, thinking it was the end. Soaked with sweat and panting, he reached up and felt of his neck and realized that he was alive. Looking around to see if anyone was there, he sat down on the bed, still shaking from his nightmare. "It was a dream, I was dreaming," he said out loud.

It took Bart about an hour to recover from his ordeal. Nightmares take a lot out of a person, but he wasn't going back to sleep for fear of another dream or the conclusion of his last dream. *I'd better go and check on J.W.,* he thought.

Wondering what the dream had meant the whole way over to J.W.'s house, Bart knew that he had been dreaming, but was still worried about his old friend. He had never had a dream so real and in the back of his mind he had doubts.

Coming up to J.W.'s house he could see J.W. on his porch and Doctor Wilson was there with him. Bart hurried up onto the porch in time to hear Doc Wilson telling J.W. "You need to take it easy for a few days and I'll be back to take the stitches out next week." J.W. was bandaged up from his shoulder to his elbow. Doctor Wilson spoke to Bart as he was leaving, "Bart, if you can stop by and check on J.W. for the next few days, maybe he'll take it easy and let those stitches do their job. That's a mighty nasty cut he has on his arm."

"I'll keep an eye on him," Bart said.

"J.W. what in the world happened to you?" asked Bart.

"Well, I was out back doing a few chores and come around the corner of the smoke house and tripped on something. The next thing I knew, I was laying on the ground, bleeding everywhere. My axe was stuck in a piece of wood and I fell on it. You know how sharp I keep my axe. It cut me pretty bad. Doc Wilson had to put in fifty stitches."

"You're lucky that you didn't cut your head or neck when you fell. At your age you're going to have to be more careful," said Bart.

"At my age! Boy, I can still move pretty good," said J.W.

"Yeah, you can," Bart said, thinking about J.W. running from the Spanish soldiers in his dream.

"Whatever happened with your trail you found?" asked J.W.

"It turned out to be nothing."

"Well, I was going to go out there and check it out myself until all this happened. It sounded real interesting."

"I just let my imagination get carried away. There ain't nothing out there," said Bart.

"You sure about that?"

"Yeah, I'm sure. Now you take care of yourself and I'll be back tomorrow to check in on you," said Bart.

"Sure will," said J.W.

Bart turned and started off of the porch to leave when he saw something shiny by the chair on the end of the porch. He walked by, but then looked back. *I didn't see what I thought I saw,* he thought, but he did. It was a Spanish soldier's metal helmet laying there on the floor. "Where did you get that?" he asked in shock. Bart gazed around at J.W., but J.W. didn't say a word. He just

sat there grinning and he was wearing buckskin
and holding a coonskin cap.

The moral of this story is …
If you stay on the beaten path,
there is much certainty.
Venturing off the path leads to discovery
and with discovery, the unknown.

Night of the Owl

It was late on a cool November night in 1964 and Nick Edwards was on his way home. Nick was eleven years old and had been squirrel hunting. Eleven seems to be very young to be hunting far from home and walking back home in the dark. But the times were hard and his family had to eat and Nick was a very capable young man. He knew that there was nothing out there to fear except fear itself.

But this night seemed strangely different to Nick. He had had a good hunt and was carrying eight gray squirrels and two red fox squirrels, all headshots except one. Nick's Grandpaw didn't want any meat wasted (which is why they were head shots), but he also liked to eat the squirrels brain and tongue. So he had to have at least one unharmed head. Nick thought that Grandpaw was hard to please. One day he asked Grandpaw if he wanted him to just shoot so close to the squirrel that he scared him to death. This earned him a whack on the head from Grandpaw's cane.

As he continued down the trail, Nick noticed that there weren't any of the usual night sounds. His footsteps seemed to echo and he hadn't even heard an owl. Nick loved to hear the owls and he could talk back to them. But tonight there were no owls, though he knew that one always hung around the little meadow. Nick tried calling to the owls, but there was no response. Then he heard a squeak and rustling in the leaves. Nick approached cautiously to see what was going on.

In the moonlight, he could see some kind of big bird lying on the ground, but it wasn't moving. Upon closer examination, Nick realized that it was a screech owl. He wondered if the owl was dead as he picked it up and realized that it was just unconscious. He felt admiration for the owl as he felt his sharp talons and looked into his big yellow eyes. Feeling that he needed to help the owl, who had apparently flown head on into the big oak tree and knocked himself out, he decided to carry it home.

Later that night, Nick had cleaned the squirrels and laid the owl on a table in his room. He was alive, but still had not come to. Nick made the owl a bed out of an old shirt and went to sleep. In the middle of the night, Nick awoke to a strange noise. The owl had woken up and was trying to fly away.

Flying into the walls and ceiling, he was injuring himself even more. Nick had to do something, so he grabbed him. This might not have been a good idea. The owl's talons were extremely sharp and dug into Nick's arm mercilessly as he tried to get a grip on the struggling bird. During all this commotion, Nick's Paw came in and turned on the light.

Paw tried to help Nick get loose from the owl, but they couldn't get the owl's talons to open up; they were locked onto Nick's arm like a pair of vise grips. Paw told Nick to hold the owl out the window and maybe it would loosen its grip. Nick didn't want to release the owl, but he did want the owl to release him. So he exchanged favors and stuck his arm out the window with the owl still attached to it. When the owl realized that it was outside, he turned loose of Nick's arm and flew up into the air. Circling twice, not knowing which way to go, it seemed as though he was looking at Nick. As the owl flew away, Nick watched him go from his window; with a very sore arm and thoughts that maybe he would see that owl again someday.

Two months later, Nick was out walking by the meadow where he had found the owl. He stopped to call, "Who cooks for you—Who cooks for you all?" and the owl answered him, "I cook for you—I cook for you all." Nick was delighted, because he loved to hear the owls talk. He took a squirrel from his game bag and tossed it toward the tree where the owl was. The squirrel never hit the ground. The owl swooped down, grabbed it and was back on the limb in three seconds. Nick was again delighted and said, "I must give you a name; I will call you Hoots because you are very good at hooting."

Soon Nick and Hoots were very close and Hoots would light on Nick's arm. Nick told his friends about Hoots and they didn't believe him. So he bet them that he could feed Hoots out of his hand. Well, they took the bet and Nick took their money. He could hold a piece of meat in his teeth, hold his head back and Hoots would snatch it clean, not even touching Nick's lips. Nick's friends couldn't believe what they saw. It was like Nick and Hoots were at one with each other in some mysterious way.

Nick and Hoots saw each other everyday. Hoots would sit outside Nick's window at night and call, "Who cooks for you—Who cooks for you all?" And Nick would call back, "I cook for you—I cook for you all." Their friendship was stronger than any he had ever had.

About a year later, one night, Nick's paw didn't come home. Nick's maw was very upset, because Paw was never late and she had supper on the table. Nick said, "I'll go find him. He was going over to Potter's place to look at some timber." "Nick, you be careful. There's moonshiners out in those woods and they don't take kindly to anyone coming around their stills."

"I will, but I have to find Paw. He could be in bad trouble," Nick grabbed his squirrel rifle and was out the door.

Nick looked and called for Hoots, but he wouldn't come. He thought that was very strange. Both Paw and Hoots were missing. Two hours later, Nick had found no sign of either one of them and had a bad feeling about this night. Knowing that the Gentry Boys had some whiskey stills down around Bear Creek, which was in the general vicinity of where Paw should have been, it would be very dangerous poking around there, but that was exactly what he was going to do.

"I've got to find Paw," he said and called for Hoots one more time: "Who cooks for you—who cooks for you all?" Instantly Hoots answered, "Who cooks for you—who cooks for you?" But that was not how Hoots usually answered. Then Hoots called again real quick, but he was not getting any closer. Hoots kept calling every minute. Nick thought, *Hoots wants me to come to him. Maybe he's found Paw.*

Nick ran most of the way, but slowed down to a sneak when he got close to Bear Creek. He could see a dim light coming from behind a small hill and detected the smell of wood smoke. Nick snuck up the hill and peeked over. There was a campfire and Hoots was in a big pine tree just behind the camp, still calling every minute:

"Who cooks for you—who cooks for you?" Then he saw Paw. He was tied to a tree and bleeding out of his mouth. The front of his shirt was covered with blood. Those Gentry boys must have beat Paw really bad. This made Nick really mad and he called to Hoots, who called right back. Paw's head came up; he knew Nick was out there.

There were three of the Gentry's sitting around the fire and they had a red hot poker stuck down in the coals. Earl Gentry (the meanest hillbilly east of the Mississippi) got up and had the hot poker in his hand. He started toward Paw and said, "I'll fix you so you won't ever talk."

Nick leveled off his squirrel rifle and shot Earl, right in the hand. The bullet went through the back of his hand, hit the steel poker and busted three of Earl's knuckles. Earl screamed and the other two hit the woods running. Nick ran down to Paw and cut him loose in a flash. Paw kicked Earl—who was down on his hands and knees screaming—right in the head and knocked him out cold.

"Let's go," he said and just as they started out of the firelight, they heard the click of a rifle hammer. They froze and slowly turned around. Both the other Gentry's were standing there and one had a rifle leveled right at them. Nick had reloaded his rifle, but he knew if he raised it, one of them would be shot. The situation looked hopeless.

"Ya'll fixin to pay now," the older Gentry said, raising the rifle and taking aim.

In desperation Nick called to Hoots, "Who cooks—who cooks." In a flash, Hoots swooped down on Gentry, sinking his talons home in Gentry's face. The other Gentry was so surprised by Hoot's attack, that it gave Nick time to raise his rifle. Recovering from his shock, the Gentry that didn't have an owl attached to his face, had drawn his knife and was closing the distance between Nick and himself.

Nick hollered, "I'll shoot!" as he took aim at Gentry's chest, but he kept coming, knife raised. Nick tried to pull the trigger, but couldn't bring himself to kill someone, while Gentry, on the other hand, would have no problem ending Nick's life.

At the last moment, Nick jumped sideways, avoiding the attack and shot Gentry in the knee. Paw grabbed the other one's rifle and broke it across his back and Hoots flew up and lit on Nick's shoulder. They stood in the firelight with all the Gentry's out cold and bleeding. Paw looked at Nick with Hoots on his shoulder and said, "Son, when we get through telling this story, it will be known forever as *The Night of the Owl.*" With that said, Paw let out a call of his own, "Who lays there—Who lays there bleeding?" and Hoots answered, "The Gentry's—The Gentry's—out cold and sleeping."

Tying the Gentrys up while they were still unconscious, Paw and Nick secured the scene. They built the fire up real big so that the Sheriff would have no trouble finding the Gentrys and their illegal whiskey making operation. With Hoots scouting the way, they headed home.

When they got there, Maw ran out crying, "I was so afraid with ya'll both out there in the night and all those owls hooting." All the owls in the countryside had been hooting all night and had suddenly stopped when Paw made his call, as if signaling that the danger was over.

From that night forward, the calls of the owls were not taken lightly, but were a constant reminder of the dangers sometimes out there and the events that had taken place on *The Night of the Owl.*

The moral of this story is …
Good overcomes evil with the courage we apply.

Turtles After School

As Tom awoke and looked out the window, he said, "Another fine day." The sun was just coming up over the mountains and shining across the waters of the Coosa River. *It sure would be a good day to catch some turtles,* he thought.

All he had to do was slip out of the house before his Maw could see him and make him go to school. He got as far as the back door when he sensed his Maw looking at him. Now that may seem strange, but he could feel her eyes on him and rather than get a good tongue lashing, he shut the door, picked up his books off of the table as if he were going to school and sure enough, when he turned around there was Maw, staring at him. "Good morning, Tom. It sure is a nice day to go to school, isn't it?" she said.

"Good morning, Maw. It sure is a nice day to catch some turtles, too."

"Yes, it is," she nodded "But you'll catch your turtles after school."

"Yes, ma'am," he said and off to school he went.

At school, Tom couldn't keep his mind off of them turtles; how many could he catch, how would he do it, how is the best way to catch them, how much money could he make selling them? His buddy, Nelson, noticed that he was preoccupied with something.

"What's on you mind, Tom?" he asked. "You have been acting mighty strange today."

"Its turtles," Tom said and went right back into his trance.

"Turtles, what turtles? You got turtles in your head?" Nelson asked with a real strange look on his face.

"No, I ain't got turtles in my head," Tom said. "Well, maybe I do have turtles in my head."

"Maybe one's in there eating away at your brain, if there's any brain left in there," Nelson laughed.

"You won't think it's funny when I catch all of them turtles and sell them. I am going to make enough money to buy me a new shotgun," Tom said excitedly.

"Won't nobody buy no turtles from you even if you do catch a whole wagon full; you're just wasting your time on another one of your bright ideas. I swear, sometimes I think you have a light bulb in your head and some voodoo witch is flipping the switch on and off," Nelson said.

"Not this time, Nelson. This time I've got a plan that will work." Nelson didn't respond to this, but decided to get away from Tom as quickly as possible, remembering the last time he got roped into one of Tom's clever schemes; he had been the laughingstock at school for a whole month because he was trying to catch birds by sprinkling salt on their tails. The old saying that if you can sprinkle salt on a bird's tail, you can catch it, is true, but finding a bird that will hold still long enough to do this, is virtually impossible.

Two days later, Nelson was going with Tom after school to catch some turtles.

"Nelson, we can go down to the Barnett Slew and set some traps. I saw a lot of loggerheads there last week," Tom said. "Then we can go over to Willow Creek and noodle for some down the creek bank."

"You sure this guy is going to buy all the turtles we catch?" Nelson asked.

"Sure he is. He carries them down to New Orleans and they make turtle soup out of them and I think they sell the claws and shells, too," Tom said.

"Okay," Nelson said. "I could use a new shotgun myself. Let's go get them snappers."

Everything went pretty well at the Barnett Slew; they set twenty or more turtle traps and felt real good about them. Tom figured they would have turtles in at least half of them.

"If we have twelve turtles in these traps tomorrow at three bucks each, that will be thirty–six dollars," Tom said. "If we do that for two weeks, we will have 360 bucks."

"Yeah, then we can both have a new shotgun *and* a new fishing pole!" Nelson said. He was getting excited about this now. "We can't let any of the other guys know about this. They will be trying to cut into our profit."

Tom said with a big smile, "By the time they catch on to us, we'll have all the turtles caught and be living the high life."

They didn't have time to noodle Willow Creek that evening, so they went home and dreamed about snapping turtles all night.

It was almost more than they could stand. They could hardly wait for school to let out. When the bell rang, they were like two wild horses, just a cloud of dust going down the trail. They came up to their first trap and there was a big old loggerhead waiting on them.

"Wow, that thing sure is mean," Nelson said.

"Yeah, and he won't turn loose until it thunders if he bites you, either," Tom said.

Well, Tom and Nelson had a day to remember. They caught eighteen snappers that evening, but they had a small problem that they hadn't counted on. They had so many turtles in the boat that Tom had to paddle while Nelson kept the snappers beat back with the other paddle. Those turtles were mad. They were snapping the boat, seats, paddle, and even each other and would be snapping Tom and Nelson if they could get to them.

"Tom, what are we going to do with all these turtles? We got to do something with them before they eat us up!" Nelson said.

"I'll think of something. Let's just get them home. I don't want to be in this boat with them after dark," Tom said. And off they went, Tom paddling like crazy and Nelson fighting off the turtles. It was a sight to behold, but there had been many such sights as far as these two were concerned. They made it back home with the turtles, and all their fingers, before dark.

"Now, what are we going to do with them?" Nelson asked. Tom had been thinking about this all the way home. Since he was the brains of the partnership, he knew he had to come up with something.

"We'll put them in the goat pen until we get ready to sell them," Tom said.

"If them turtles eat them goats, we'll be in a heap of trouble," Nelson said.

"Turtles can't eat goats, Nelson. The goats are way too fast. They'll just jump out of the way." Sure enough, the snappers tried to snap the goats, but the goats just jumped out of the way. As a matter of fact, the goats seemed to like playing with the turtles.

Well, the turtle trapping went on like this for a whole week. Tom and Nelson were so tired that they could hardly stay awake during school. This had turned into a big job and they hadn't had time to noodle Willow Creek like Tom had planned. The goat pen was full of loggerhead turtles and something had to be done with them, because the goats were running out of room to dodge the angry snappers.

It was Friday morning and Tom and Nelson had just gotten to school.

"Nelson, it's time to sell turtles. You know what that means," Tom said.

"Yeah, it means that the goats will survive, which means that we will survive without getting our hides tanned."

"No, no, no," Tom said. "It means that we are going to make some dough! It means that we will be the richest boys in town. It means that all the girls will be chasing us and we can just pick the ones we want and shake off the rest. We may even get our pictures in the newspaper and a story on our business. Nelson, this is going to be our first step to becoming Turtle Tycoons! We could control all the turtle trade in the United States."

"Hold on, Tom. You're getting just a slight bit carried away. I'll be satisfied with a new shotgun and new fishing pole and one or maybe two girlfriends that don't think they have to boss me around. But I don't want to be a Turtle Tycoon," Nelson said.

"Well, you don't have to be a Tycoon. You can just catch them and I'll buy them from you. Then I'll ship them over to New Orleans and I'll be the Tycoon. 'Tom, the Turtle Tycoon.' That sounds pretty good, or T.T.T for short. You can call me Mr. T, yeah that's it. Call me Mr. T now, so I can hear how it sounds."

"That's enough. I ain't calling you Mr. T and if I did the T would be short for trouble. I'll see you in the morning," Nelson said.

The next morning, Tom and Nelson met at the goat pen. They didn't know exactly how many turtles they had in the pen and had tried to count them several times without any luck. "Tom, we've got to figure out how many turtles we have. They won't hold still long enough to count them and I don't want to get cheated out of one single turtle. We worked too hard," Nelson said.

"I've got it all figured out," Tom said. "I've got this piece of chalk and all we've got to do is number each turtle, until we get them all marked. Then, we'll know exactly how many we've got." They started numbering the turtles while trying to avoid their snapping jaws. The count came up to eighty–four.

"That's more than I thought we'd have," Nelson said excitedly.

"Nelson, at three bucks a turtle that's 252 dollars. *We're in the money, we're in the money…* " Tom sang. "We'll be hunting rabbits with brand new Remingtons this year. I'll tell you, Nelson, this turtle trapping is hard work, but the pay off is worth the effort."

The boys got everything in order while they waited on the turtle truck to arrive. They even tied short pieces of rope to the legs of the meanest snappers, so they would be easy to handle. Tom made out an invoice with the number of turtles and the amount of money they would bring. As a matter of fact, they were handling their business affairs quite well.

The turtle truck pulled up in a cloud of dust as they anxiously waited. A big man with huge hands and fingers stepped out of the truck.

"Hello, Tom. I hope you have as many turtles as you told me you would, because I've got a lot of hungry folks down in New Orleans and they can hardly wait for some Alabama turtle soup."

"Well, we've got more than I told you I could catch," Tom smiled.

"Look at his hands, Tom," Nelson stammered. "I ain't never seen hands so big; his thumb is four times as big as mine."

"Quit gawking, Nelson. This is Mr. Lutz and he's going to buy our turtles, so don't offend him," Tom said.

"You won't offend me," Mr. Lutz said. "I've heard about everything and it takes a lot to get under my skin. Besides, these big hands come in handy when dealing with turtles." Mr. Lutz stuck out his hand to Nelson.

Nelson reluctantly reached out for Mr. Lutz's hand: not because he didn't like him, but because the size of his hand intimidated him. "Nice to meet you Mr. Lutz." His hand was swallowed by the turtle handler's hand and the only thing Nelson could think was, *This man could hit me with his thumb and knock me cold.*

Mr. Lutz and the boys started loading the turtles in the truck. Tom and Nelson were doubling up on the big, mean snappers, while Mr. Lutz was slinging turtles in that truck two at a time. He was grabbing them around the shell and palming them with those big hands like a basketball player palming a basketball. In a few minutes they had them all loaded up except for one.

"You ought to leave one in there for the goats to play with," Mr. Lutz said. He knew what he was talking about, because those goats were already jumping and dodging that snapper. They were having a big 'ole time.

"Tom, you and Nelson did real well. I had my doubts about you when you first told me how many you could catch, but I see you are a man of your word."

"Thanks, Mr. Lutz. We sure appreciate the business," Tom said.

"Yeah, thanks," Nelson spurted out. "Are you coming back to buy some more turtles when we catch them?"

"Sure," Mr. Lutz said with a smile. "I'll be looking forward to seeing ya'll again. By the way, if ya'll know where you can catch one of those huge alligator snapping turtles, and I mean a big one, I've got a guy that runs a zoo over in Baton Rouge who is looking for one. There would be a big bonus for one in the hundred pound range."

"I know where four or five of them are," Tom started. "We're going noodling over at Willow Creek next week and there are a few over there."

"You boys be careful," Mr. Lutz warned. "A turtle that size can hurt a man. I knew of a trapper down in the bayou that grabbed hold of the wrong end of one. His partner said it dragged him down and he never came up. If you are going to get in the water with him, have a rope tied to you so your partner can pull you out. Always have a knife on you, too. That way, if he pulls you down, you can poke his eyes out and he'll let you go."

"I ain't getting in the water with one of them," Nelson chattered.

"I'll do it," Tom said, without any fear in his voice. "You just hold the end of the rope in case I get in trouble."

"You're not afraid of those big snappers?" Mr. Lutz asked.

"No," Tom said quite frankly. "Paw taught us that the only thing to fear is fear itself. He taught us to respect things and know what they can do, but it doesn't do much good to fear because fear will make you hurt yourself."

Mr. Lutz replied, "It sounds like your Paw was a smart man. See you boys next week." And he drove off in a cloud of dust, headed for New Orleans with a truck load of snappers.

After counting and dividing their money, Tom and Nelson were on cloud nine because they had never had this much money before. They had sold some catfish and done odd jobs, but had never imagined finding a gold mine in snapping turtles.

"Tom, I have to hand it to you on this one. I had my doubts, but this turtle idea of yours has really paid off," Nelson said.

"Why, thank you, Nelson," Tom said. "I really appreciate you being my partner and acknowledging my intellect. Now I wish you would just call me Mr. T, so I can hear how it sounds from someone who admires me so much."

"I knew I shouldn't have paid you a compliment; all it does is go to your big head. You can take your Mr. T and sit on it, because I ain't gonna call you nothing, but a big 'ole fat head. Now, I am going to go hide my money and I'll see you Monday," Nelson said with an irritated look on his face.

"What about tomorrow?"

"I have got to have a day off and if you know what's good for you, you'll get rested up so we can catch one or two of those alligator snapping turtles," Nelson said.

"Okay, Okay," Tom said. "We'll take a day off, so we don't violate your union contract, but come prepared for big turtles on Monday."

Well, Tom and Nelson enjoyed their day off. All those turtles had taken a toll on them. Both of them slept all day long, but come Monday, they were all fired up and ready to go. Tom met Nelson in front of the school an hour early, so they could make plans for that afternoon. The boys had everything nearly worked out when Earl and

Joe Walker came up and they had to cut it off short.

"What you boys got going on?" Earl asked. "Ya'll been keeping to yourselves and acting mighty secretive."

"It ain't none of your business," Nelson spouted.

"Well, we might make it our business," Earl said.

Now Earl was mean as a snake and loved to fight and Nelson wasn't going to back down either. So, Tom figured he'd better smooth things out a little before the cat got out of the bag. With him being the brains of this outfit, it was his obligation to keep this project incognito.

Although I wouldn't mind seeing Nelson knot up Earl's head, Tom thought to himself.

"Hold up there," Tom said. "No need in anybody getting their feathers ruffled, especially this early in the morning. Ya'll would have to sit in school all day with blood and dust all over you and knots on your head and that wouldn't be a pleasant day." Tom was trying to stall until he could think up some way out of this situation.

"We've just been talking about that new girl that came to school today."

"There ain't no new girl here. We're the only ones here, you knuckle head," Earl said.

"I mean the new girl that's going to come to school today. I saw her this weekend and she sure is pretty."

"All right," Earl said. "But ya'll better watch your step or I'll put a whipping on you that you can't wash off with your momma's lye soap." Nelson just stared at him with fire in his eyes. Joe turned around and grinned at Nelson as they walked off. That really made Nelson mad and Tom had to grab him by the arm to hold him back.

"What are you trying to do?" Nelson barked. "I was fixing to whip him good."

"I know you were," Tom said. "But we got to keep a low profile, at least until we catch and sell all those turtles. Then I'll help you. I can take Joe while you handle Earl—if you can."

"Well, I can and then I'll take care of you, too, and I'll do it all before breakfast!" Tom started laughing. He loved to get Nelson riled up and was quite good at it.

"And what do you mean telling them a new girl is coming to school today? You ain't seen no new girl. We been too busy and if you had seen a pretty girl, you wouldn't tell nobody. You're going to blow our cover for sure," Nelson said angrily. He was still fired up.

"No, I didn't see a new girl, but I did hear Maw talking about the Stamps' having a cousin move in with them and that she was about our age," Tom said.

"Well, she can't be too pretty if she's a Stamps," Nelson said. "They sure weren't blessed with good looks."

"No they weren't," Tom said "And Earl and Joe weren't blessed with much brains either."

"No they weren't," Nelson said and they laughed as they walked into school.

Class started and there was no new girl. Earl looked around and thought that Tom had lied to him. He was shaking his fist at Tom when she came through the door. All the guys just stared at her as she walked up to Miss Wilson's desk.

"Class, this is Eleanor Stamps and she will be attending school here for the rest of the year," Miss Wilson said. "I want everyone to be nice to her and make her feel right at home." Tom didn't hear a word that Miss Wilson had said. All he could think of was how beautiful Eleanor was. He had never seen a girl this pretty.

Nelson saw Tom's jaw hanging down and thought to himself, *Here we go again. He's done fell for her and he just saw her. No more turtles, no more money, no more fun. Earl's probably going to kill him and everything is ruined now.* Tom couldn't take his eyes or his brain off of Eleanor and Nelson was getting sick of it.

"Tom, snap out of it," Nelson said. "We got this turtle business to take care of."

"What turtles?" Tom breathed out slowly.

"Those big alligator snappers. You know, the one's we're going to get a big bonus for."

"What bonus?" Tom asked blankly.

Nelson knew that there was big trouble brewing. Tom had lost all of his senses and he was the brains of this partnership. He had to snap the love sick Turtle Tycoon out of his trance.

"The bonus we're going to get so you can have extra money to buy Eleanor flowers and to buy Eleanor presents and to carry Eleanor out on a date," said Nelson trying to get into Tom's head. "Boy, she sure will be impressed by all that money you're going to have. She won't have anything to do with any of those other poor bums except, maybe me," Nelson grinned. That last phrase did the job.

"You back off Nelson. I saw her first!" Tom said with fire in his eyes.

"I'll back off if you'll get your mind back on our business," Nelson countered.

"Okay, okay, let's get back to business. Anyway, she probably won't even talk to any of those guys. They're not nearly as good looking or as charming as I am," Tom said with a grin.

Tom and Nelson made it through the day at school and set off for Willow Creek. When they got there, things didn't look so good. The creek was really muddy and swift.

"Man, we ain't going to find no turtles in there," Nelson said. Tom didn't reply. He was just looking and studying the creek trying to figure out how they could catch a turtle in that mess. He had made a promise that he could catch one or two of those big alligator snappers and Mr. Lutz wouldn't be very happy if they came in empty handed.

"I think we'll have to stick find them," Tom said.

"What do you mean, stick find them? We can't see anything in that muddy water," said Nelson.

"You sure are right about that," Tom said. "We'll cut us some cane poles and poke around on the bottom until we hit his shell and then, all we've got to do is get a rope on him and pull him out."

"Simple as that," Nelson said sarcastically. "Put the rope on him and pull him right on out. Maybe we can tap on his shell and he'll stick up his head and say, 'Who's there?' and we'll say, 'Got,' and he'll say, 'Got who?' and we'll say, 'Got you,' put the rope around his head, pull him out and be on our merry way!"

"Well, not exactly like that, but almost," said Tom. "First, we have to find one, and then we locate the business end and dive down and put a rope on his tail. Let's go down to the big bend. There's an eddy just below the bend and with this strong current, that's probably where he's at. He could just lay there and catch his food as it washed by."

The boys found some canes growing on the creek bank and cut four good long ones. When they got to the bend in the creek, there was an eddy just like Tom had said there would be.

"You were right," Nelson said. "He's probably laying right there in that slack water and he's probably got his mouth wide open waiting for a minnow or a fish or somebody's leg." Tom was getting excited and Nelson was getting worried. He didn't like the idea of getting in that muddy water and he didn't like the look in Tom's eyes.

"Nelson, you stand on that high bank with the rope and the poles," Tom said. "I'll wade in from down below. If he's here, he's facing upstream." Nelson felt a sigh of relief.

"I'll wade in there if you don't want to," Nelson said, not really wanting to, but just trying to act like a man.

"Well, you could, I guess," Tom said, and Nelson could feel his stomach knotting up. "But I'd rather you hold the rope. When I get him tied on, he'll be real mad and that's when you'll earn your pay. You've got to hold him off of me until I get out of the water."

Tom waded in with one of the poles, slowly searching the bottom for the big turtle. He bumped something that felt like a tail and gently eased up a little further.

"I feel his shell," Tom said and stuck the pole up in the mud by the snapper's tail. "Give me another pole." Nelson tossed him another pole and Tom gently ran the pole down the turtle's back and stuck it on the other side of the turtle.

"All right, Nelson, give me the end of the rope." Nelson tied a slip knot in the end and tossed it to Tom. "You might want to wrap the rope around that tree. This is a big turtle and you wouldn't want him to pull you in."

Nelson wrapped the rope around the tree and said, "Okay, I'm ready. How are you going to get the rope on him?"

"I'm going to dive down, find the end of his tail and gently slide the loop onto it. You watch the poles while I'm down there. He'll knock them down when he spins around. Then you've really got to pull, because when I tighten that loop on his tail, he'll be coming after me."

"Tom, you be real careful. If he gets a hold of you, you're turtle meat," Nelson warned.

"I know. I'm a little scared to do this. Maybe you had better do it and I'll hold the rope," Tom said with a grin.

Nelson knew he was kidding. He had never seen Tom back down from anything because he was scared. Tom was still grinning when he went under with the rope. He slid his hand down the pole that was stuck beside the turtle's tail until he could feel it. Slowly he ran his fingers down the tail to the tip. The whole time he was thinking, *This tail is huge. I hope Nelson can hold him off long enough for me to get out of the water.*

Well, Tom slipped the loop over the tail and clinched it tight. Boy, that snapper did not like that. Nelson saw the poles go down and tightened up on the rope. Just then Tom came out from under the water in reverse. He was high stepping out of that water when he thought he stepped on a large boulder. Then the boulder moved and he felt the snapper's head snap right beside his foot.

"There're two of them!" he shouted as he leaped out of the water.

"I can't hold him!" Nelson hollered. The rope was sliding around the tree and dragging Nelson with it.

"Hold on!" Tom shouted. "We can't let this bad boy get away!" Tom grabbed the rope and they stopped it from sliding any more. Just then, the turtle came to the surface and boy was he mad. If that wasn't enough, the other turtle came up and they each thought it was the other one that had disturbed them. The fight was on. They were snapping at each other like crazy with heads as big as basketballs and powerful jaws that could remove a man's hand from his arm. Then they locked up mouth to mouth, one had a death grip on the other and the other had a death grip on him. Tom and Nelson looked at each other in total amazement.

With the two turtles locked up like that, they didn't fight against the rope as hard.

"All right, Nelson, let's drag 'em in!" Tom said. They got the turtles up on the bank and they still had a hold of each other.

"We got em, now what are we going to do with em?" Nelson pouted. Tom didn't have a quick answer for that one. There was no way that they could drag them home one at a time, much less with two of them locked together.

"Come on, Tom, you got to think of something!" Nelson shouted.

"All right," Tom said. "First, we got to get a rope on the other one's tail and tie them to a tree, so we can get a breather." It wasn't hard to do that with the turtle's locked together because they weren't turning loose until it thundered.

Now, both turtles were tied up and the boys sat down to catch their breath. "Man, those turtles have got to weigh two hundred pounds apiece," Tom said. "Can you imagine how big of a bonus we'll get for four hundred pounds of turtle?"

"Yes, I can," Nelson said. "A big one!" Tom went over to the turtle and there was something sticking out of his shell. It looked like a piece of stone, so he took his knife and dug it out.

"Nelson, this is an arrowhead," Tom said holding the piece of flint up for Nelson to see. "This arrowhead must be three to five hundred years old. I wonder how old this turtle is?"

"I don't know," Nelson said. "But I guess those Indians liked to eat turtle just like those folks down in New Orleans."

"I guess," Tom said. "But they didn't eat this one."

Tom and Nelson sat there looking at the old turtle when Nelson said, "Tom, you know what we got to do," while he was staring at the turtle. Tom could see it in his face.

"Yep, I do. That old boy survived the Indians and no telling what else some three or four hundred years ago. He made it a lot farther than George Custard did at Little Big Horn. There ain't no way we're going to do him in. Besides, we can get by with one big bonus if we can get the other one home."

With that they untied the turtle, but he still had a death grip on the other one.

"Now, what are we going to do? Sit here until a storm comes, so it can thunder, so they will turn loose of each other?" Nelson asked.

"No, no, no," Tom said. "I have a little trick to get them apart. I can take a piece of pine straw, stick it down his nostrils and he'll turn loose."

"No, you can't. You couldn't pull them apart with two horses. There's no way a piece of pine straw will get them apart," Nelson said a little irritated.

"I'll show you, but don't show anybody else, because this is a secret that my Grandpaw taught me."

Tom found some long pieces of pine straw and eased up to the turtles. He sat down and crossed his legs right there beside them.

"Get back you idiot. If they do turn loose, they will get a hold of you!" Nelson warned. Tom paid Nelson no attention at all. He was focused totally on those turtles. Looking into their eyes as if he was going inside of them, slowly he took a straw and slid it down the old turtle's nostril. The old turtle loosened his grip. Nelson was nervous as a cat. Both turtles were loose with those killer jaws wide open and Tom was still sitting right there beside them.

The old turtle turned his head toward Tom, but he didn't snap him. It was as if he was looking into Tom's eyes. Then he turned his head and crawled back into the water. Maybe he realized that he had dodged another bullet and simply went on his way. Now the other turtle turned his head toward Tom and there was no love in his eyes. In a split second Tom realized that he was going to snap him. He rolled back just as the turtle struck. The turtle grabbed his shoe by the heel and luckily his foot slid right out of his shoe. Nelson was breathing so hard that he couldn't talk and Tom just rolled over and laid there on the ground. It would have made a good picture. The boys all tuckered out and a two hundred pound snapping turtle sitting there with a shoe in his mouth.

Tom sat up and said, "Nelson, how about going over there and getting my shoe for me?"

Nelson looked at the turtle and then looked at Tom. Both of them busted out laughing.

"You might as well give him the other shoe and go barefoot," Nelson said.

"I believe you are correct, Nelson. Let's get this grumpy old boy home. I've had about enough excitement for today, but we'll have to come up with something for tomorrow," said Tom.

Now they had a problem. They couldn't drag the turtle because he would just dig his claws in the ground and wouldn't budge. He was too heavy to carry and neither of the boys wanted to handle him too close because he was really agitated.

After about an hour had gone by, things weren't looking so good. The turtle hadn't budged one inch. Tom reached down and grabbed the turtle's tail and pulled up on it. The turtle took a step forward. Tom did it again and the turtle took another step forward. Tom exclaimed, "I've got it. We'll make him walk, just like Paw would make them mules walk when they would sulk on him."

"I don't think that hitting that turtle in the head with a two by four is going to make him walk," Nelson said.

"No, not that way," Tom said. "We'll tie a rope on each of his front feet and one onto his tail. We can guide him with the two front ropes and put him in gear by pulling up on his tail." Nelson had his doubts about this working, but they went ahead with it and tied the ropes like Tom had prescribed.

"Let's carry him back to the barn," Tom said, raising the turtle's tail with the rope. Sure enough, the turtle started walking and the boys just had to guide him with the side ropes. Now this was a strange sight and when they got the turtle home, Tom's Maw thought they had captured a dinosaur.

"Saints alive, Tom, you've caught a monster! I ain't never seen anything like that!" said Tom's Maw.

"It's just a little snapping turtle Maw. We let the big one go," Tom said with a grin.

"You're just as bad as your Grand–paw and Paw. No, you're even crazier than they are!" Maw said and turned to go into the house shaking her head and murmuring something under her breath.

"Nelson, you wanna have some fun?" Tom asked. "Let's walk this old boy right through the middle of town."

"Good idea," Nelson said. "We've got to show him off. The mayor may even give us some kind of award for catching the world's largest turtle."

"Now you're thinking like me," Tom said.

"Yeah, that could be dangerous," Nelson said. Both of them laughed and headed the turtle up the road toward town with Tom's shoe still in his mouth.

When they came into town, it wasn't long before a big crowd gathered around them and followed them down the street. Everyone was amazed at the sight of such a big turtle. The newspaper reporter was writing their story down on a pad. The headline would read, "Two Young Adventurers Escape the Jaws of Death!" and there was a picture on the front page of Tom and Nelson on each side of the snapper, with the shoe still in his mouth and Tom barefooted. They saw Earl and Joe Walker, who were trying to be buddy–buddy with them, now that they were famous. Then they saw Mr. and Mrs. Stamps and Eleanor was with them. She looked in awe at that big ole turtle and then looked at Nelson and smiled. Tom couldn't stand it because she didn't even notice him.

"Hey, Nelson," Eleanor said, "You must be very brave to catch a turtle like that." Nelson was grinning from ear to ear.

"It ain,t nothing much. I just used Tom's foot for bait and when he bit down on his shoe; I just pulled him free and saved his life." Nelson was laying it on heavy.

Tom spoke up, "Well, how are you going to get my shoe back, Nelson? I'll have to go barefoot if you don't and my feet are getting a little sore." Tom figured that would fix him good, but Nelson stepped right up.

"I'll get it back for you right now if I can borrow that straw Mr. Stamps is chewing on."

"Sure, boy, here," Mr. Stamps said and handed him the straw.

Now, there was a big crowd gathered to see this and if Nelson could pull it off, he would be "The Man." Nelson sat down right in front of the turtle and Eleanor gasped, "Be careful, Nelson." Nelson grinned at Tom and Tom decided that he might as well help him since Eleanor didn't even know that he was there.

"Everyone be quiet. The least distraction could cause Nelson to lose a hand or arm."

Now everybody was in a trance, eyes wide and mouths open and Nelson was doing quite well. If he was nervous, it didn't show. Slowly he reached up and got hold of the shoe. With the other hand he slid the straw down the turtle's nostril. The turtle loosened his grip and hissed with his mouth wide open. Nelson pulled the shoe out and saw danger in the snapper's eyes. He knew he had to act fast. He tossed the shoe toward Tom and rolled in the other direction as the turtle watched the shoe. But the snapper turned back to Nelson and struck out at him, just barely missing his behind as he rolled out of the way. His jaws came together with such force that it sounded like two hammers hitting. Everyone jumped back a step or two, the men hollered and the women screamed.

Nelson had done it. Everyone was cheering for him and slapping him on the back. Eleanor ran up to him and gave him a big hug. The news reporter had snapped a picture just as the turtle had snapped at Nelson. Nelson was famous and

Tom got his shoe back, although it was nearly bitten in half.

After all the smoke had cleared, Tom and Nelson were walking the turtle back home when Tom said, "Well, Nelson, looks like you're going to be the Tycoon. I guess I should be calling you Mr. T from now on."

Nelson looked at Tom and said with a big grin on his face, "Naw, you deserve to be the Tycoon, Tom. I'll just be the hero." Both of them laughed as they headed down the road.

Mr. Lutz came the next day to pick up the turtle and was amazed at the size of that snapper.

"You boys have done real well," he said. "I think that this turtle will be the biggest in captivity. Here's $1,000 and I'll send you the rest of it when I get him to the zoo. I don't know how much more it will be, but it will be at least double that." The boys later received $2,000 more from Mr. Lutz. They were in all the papers, outdoor magazines, and there was even a T.V. crew that came and made a documentary on them. They were living the high life and enjoying every minute of it. Nelson and Eleanor hit it off real well. Tom became known as "The Turtle Tycoon" and everyone was happy.

J

After a few months, though, something was missing. There wasn't any sense of adventure anymore. Turtling had turned into a job, Tom was restless and Nelson was getting hen pecked by Eleanor. Tom told Nelson one evening, "Nelson, I need some adventure, some excitement."

Nelson replied, "Yeah, I know what you mean. We need another adventure."

"Yeah, I think I'll make a list of things that we can do," Tom said. "How do you spell alligator, with one L or two?" Nelson looked at Tom and had to smile. He could see the wheels turning in Tom's head and knew that it wouldn't be long until they were back in action.

The moral of this story is ...
Seek adventure if you dare,
but beware the danger in the air.

Story Teller

Dick Bennett sat on the bench just outside the barber shop as he did almost every morning of the week. Dick was eighty–nine years old and had lived a very exciting and memorable life. Now, his eyes didn't see very well, nor did his ears hear very well. His bones and joints were stiff and had to be warmed up before he made his daily walk downtown. Things just didn't happen as quick for him anymore, but they did happen. Dick Bennett wasn't going to lay down until he was laid in the ground to rest.

You see, Dick Bennett had a gift and he didn't mind using it. His memory was very good and his ability to tell stories was alluring to both old and young. He was the town's storyteller and someone always seemed to be hanging around just to see what he would say next.

One day, Ed the barber didn't have any customers and stepped outside to speak to Dick.

"Good morning, Mr. Bennett," Ed spoke respectfully.

"Morning Ed. Looks like we are going to have another fine day," Dick smiled as he spoke to Ed. His face wrinkled up from years of smiling and brown as old leather from his many adventures under the sun.

"Every day is always another nice day to you. How do you keep such an optimistic outlook all the time?" asked Ed.

"Well, I came to a realization when I was a young man that really opened my eyes. I don't know why I could see it so clearly. Maybe the Good Lord just plastered it in front of me. Many people go through life and never even catch a glimpse of it."

"Of what?" asked Ed. Dick had already captured his attention in less than thirty seconds and you could see the anticipation in Ed's eyes.

"Happiness," Dick paused, "Happiness keeps you healthy and gives you a reason to live. Life throws us curves and we deal with them as best we can, but happiness gives us the drive to live; the drive to seek adventure and companionship. You just have to get your mind right."

"That makes sense to me, but how did you get your mind right?" asked Ed in earnest.

Jim Wilkins, the pharmacist, stepped out of the Drug Store for a break and saw Dick and Ed sitting on the bench. Jim walked over and said, "Morning fellows."

"Morning Jim," was the reply from both men. Dick went on with his story as Jim sat down on the bench.

"Well, I grew up down on the banks of the Coosa River. We really had it good back then. Hunting, fishing, swimming, farming, what more could a young man want?"

"One morning I woke up, poured a cup of coffee and went out on the porch to watch the sun come up. Paw was already out there. I never could manage to get up and about before him. I guess that was a feeling of security to me, knowing that he was already there. We'd say good morning and then sit there watching the sun come up and he would give me instructions on what needed to be done that day. It might be, *'We need some meat today,'* which meant I could go hunting or fishing or *'the garden needed weeding,'* which meant some hard work."

"On that particular morning, it was *'the garden needed weeding.'* That wasn't what I wanted to hear. I still remember hearing the bullfrogs croaking that morning and a whippoorwill singing his lonely song. I just knew the fish would be biting. You know the old saying was that when you hear the bullfrogs, that means the fish are biting and when there was a whippoorwill in combination with the frogs that meant the fish were biting like crazy and the whippoorwill was calling for someone to come catch them. So I really didn't want to work in the garden that day."

Jim and Ed were sitting on the edge of their seats. Every word that Dick spoke was funneling through their minds. Andy walked up from the hardware store and said,

"Morning men. Looks like ya'll are planning to save the world."

"Dick was just telling us a story," said Ed as Andy joined them and Dick continued.

"I sat there looking out over the water and could almost see those big bass striking my lure. It was such a beautiful morning and our garden was so big. By the time I finished, it would be dark. I kept dwelling on how much I didn't want to work that garden. So I told Paw, 'Listen to those bullfrogs. Today is the best looking day to go fishing that I've seen all year and we've got a fish fry coming up next month, don't we?'

'Yep,' said Paw. 'Gonna be a big one too. I bet there will be fifty people here.'"

"I saw that as an opportunity to get out of working the garden that day. I told Paw that maybe I should go fishing that day and take care of the garden the next day. It made perfect sense to me, but Paw didn't think so. 'Nope,' he said. 'The garden needs weeding today. You can go fishing tomorrow.'"

As Dick paused to take a drink of water, Harry Morethan, the self appointed mayor, saw that something was going on where the men were gathering. Harry, always thinking about votes, thought that he should ease on over there and check things out.

"Good morning, gentlemen," said Harry in his best political voice. All the men looked up and Dick said, "Morning, mayor."

Ed chimed in, "Dick was telling us a story about being happy. Maybe you should listen and then, maybe you can do something for this town that will make us happy." All the men laughed except Harry, but he took it on the chin and decided to join them. The bench was full now and some more people had gathered around as Dick continued his story.

"Well, when Paw said, 'Nope' it was more than I could stand. In my mind, I could hear the frogs getting louder and the fish were jumping out of the water laughing at me. My head felt like it was going to explode. That's when it happened." You could hear a pin drop it was so quiet as Dick paused to look around at all the people and see the expressions on their faces.

"That's when what happened?" Jim blurted out, wanting to rush Dick on with his story. Jim had some medicine to sell, but he had a problem and Dick knew it as he looked in Jim's eyes. Jim had gotten so involved in the story that he couldn't leave without knowing how the story ended.

"I lost all control. The pressure was so great, I just went crazy. I don't think that I was foaming at the mouth, but I may have been. I jumped up and started hollering at Paw. 'I'm not weeding that stupid garden today. I'm going fishing and there is nothing that you can do about it!'"

"Paw had stood with his coffee in his right hand and I didn't even see his left hand move as he walloped me square on the chin. I remember flying backwards and landing on my back on the porch. All I could see was stars. The laughing of the frogs and fish had stopped. I could hear Paw's voice like it was coming from some distant place. 'Son, there's things that a man wants to do and there's things that a man has to do.' Then everything went black."

"When I came to, I was lying in the garden on my back. I turned my head from side to side and was surrounded by corn. Paw had dragged me around to the garden, showing me the error of my ways and when I came to I didn't have a problem understanding. Not even thinking about going fishing, I got to my feet and there was a hoe laying there in front of me." Dick paused for a minute, rubbing his chin as though he was thinking.

"What did you do then?" Ed pleaded. "Well, I started hoeing the garden of course. I wasn't dwelling on the fact that I had to work in the garden instead of going fishing. When I got it all finished, I stood back and looked at what I had done. It gave me a great sense of accomplishment and I smiled, although my lips were a little sore. Ever since then, I have tried to smile and find something good about every day. There was no more dwelling on negativities for me, no sir."

Dick stopped talking and there was silence. Everyone there was waiting for him to say something else and they were all wondering if that was the end of Dick's story. Dick sat there quiet as a mouse, knowing someone would break the silence. Ed couldn't stand it any longer.

"Dick, when did you see it?"

"See what?" Dick asked.

"You know, happiness," Ed said.

"Oh that—well I saw it when Paw knocked the dwelling out of me." There was a few seconds of silence as Dick sat there grinning, then at once everyone laughed and went on their own way.

After everyone had dispersed, Dick sat there on the bench, reminiscing about his Paw and what he had done for him that morning. Mrs. Jones, the town busybody, walked by and said, "What are you grinning about Dick Bennett?"

"Good morning, Mrs. Jones. I was just thinking about a lesson learned long ago and one of my most memorable fishing trips on the very next day." Dick stood up and politely offered Mrs. Jones a seat on the bench.

"Would you like to join me?" Dick offered with a sparkle in his eyes and a smile on his face.

The moral of this story is …
Haste not to dwell on the darkness of the day,
but rush forth in pursuit of happiness.

Snakes Alive

It came gliding down the river bank, stopping every few seconds to listen and test the air with his tongue for any signs of food. It could hear water splashing up ahead, which is a sure sign of something to eat. Closer and closer it came, always searching with its tongue, for some sign of what was up ahead. Now, there were strange sounds that it could not identify. It kept coming right along, silent as the water that it swam in. Its big head rising above the water with eyes fixed ahead that looked like the devil himself—A deadly picture of evil.

Closer to the source of the splashing, it went into sneak mode. It opened its cotton lined mouth to loosen up its fangs. His venom pockets were full, ready to inject a lethal dose into anything edible, or anything else that got in the way.

Now, it could see movement up ahead, a little boy and little girl playing and splashing in the edge of the water. Its motivation was very simple; bite, kill, eat and defend was its being. Closer now and readying for the strike, silent death was upon the children and they were unaware. It flexed its jaws once again to fill the fangs with venom. It struck with deadly intention, but missed its mark. Everything was dark and its life was being choked from it. The children had run up on the bank and now were out of harm's way.

"Snakes alive!" screamed the mother of the children, who was also the mother of the young man who had just jumped from his perch above onto the head of the large cottonmouth moccasin, ending his deadly assault on his little brother and sister.

Jesse came out of the water holding the five foot long cottonmouth by the head.

"Snakes alive!" his Maw screamed again. "Kill that thing; it's the devil."

"Now, Maw," Jesse said. "All snakes are not bad."

"Jesse Merrell, you do something with that snake now." Jesse took a good look at the snake, studying it from head to tail. Beginning with its dark tail and just above that was the scent hole where it was secreting a foul smelling, cream looking fluid. Up its massive, muscular body to an oversized head, which was an evil sight, wide and muscular with pits and nostrils. Eyes so wicked that you don't even want to look into them, and the inside of its mouth, white as cotton. Jesse knew that the white mouth was part of its defense. When the cottonmouth opens its mouth at you, it means back up and sometimes it means run because they will come after you.

Other than the eyes, the fangs were the next scariest part of the snake. Three quarters of an inch long and bigger around than a needle. Curved in a slight arch, so it could hold whatever it bites long enough to inject the lethal venom. This one had double fangs on one side. The fangs were so big that it would hurt really bad to be bitten even without any venom. The venom, if it doesn't kill you, will rot the flesh around the bite. Jesse had seen people bitten on the leg and have a big sunk–in hole where the venom had rotted the muscle tissue. Yep, this is one bad boy.

"Jesse, I've done told you once!" his Maw said, holding a stick and shaking it at him. "Or I'll beat it to death with you holding it!" Jesse figured that he had pushed it far enough. He tossed the snake straight up in the air, catching it by the tail on its way down and with one smooth motion, popping the snake like someone snapping a bullwhip. He popped the head right off and it went sailing out into the bushes.

"Thank you," his Maw said. "Now hang that snake in a tree so it will rain. We need a rain real bad." Jesse did as his Maw said and they started back to the house, which you could see from the river. It was back just far enough that the flood waters couldn't reach it when the river flooded.

They lived on the middle section of the Coosa River, which was a great place for a boy to grow up. There was always something to do; Jesse had never been bored in his entire life. There was always work around the farm and always some kind of excitement around the river.

Jesse was nineteen years old and had been catching snakes since he was ten. Snakes just seemed to fascinate him and he had built quite a reputation around the county as a snake catcher. People would call him to remove snakes from their property, which was right up his alley, and it kept him supplied with spending money, because people would pay to have snakes removed. Jesse had it figured that ninety percent of people were scared of snakes, that nine percent weren't scared, but kept their distance, and one percent had no fear of snakes at all. Half of that one percent were usually idiots and the other half just understood snakes and respected what they could do.

Jesse always told people that a snake was like a sharp knife. He would say, "That knife will cut you real bad and you know it will. Therefore, you don't take it and slice your arm off. A snake will bite you sometimes and sometimes it won't. As long as you don't catch the snake by the mouth with some part of your body, you're okay. Most of the time, it is people's fear of snakes that cause them to get hurt.

Evening came and Jesse's maw had supper on the table. Jesse's Maw was one fine cook and he had no trouble showing up at the dinner table. Jesse's Paw and Maw, his little brother, Sam and his little sister, Jean, were all at the table. There was a deer roast, turnip greens, corn, okra, tomatoes, and cornbread, and it was all good. The Merrell's worked hard to make a living and put food on the table and they really enjoyed eating. Of course, having a cook like Jesse's maw had a lot to do with that.

"Was that thunder?" asked Jesse's paw.

"Yes, it was," said Maw. "Jesse hung a great big cottonmouth in a tree this morning."

"That will do it every time," Paw said. "I guess it didn't have a head on it either." Jesse just shook his head and grinned.

"Boy, you're going to have to teach me how to do that one day," Paw said.

"Sure, Paw," said Jesse. "But there is one slight problem."

"What's that son?" Paw asked.

"Well, you've actually got to touch the snake to pop his head off," Jesse said, and they all laughed. Jesse's paw was a brave man, but thought that snakes were evil and wouldn't touch one with a stick, much less his hand.

Well it rained and it rained and it rained. After two days, it finally stopped and the river was rising fast. Paw told Jesse, "You better get down there and get that snake out of that tree before we all drown."

"Yes, sir," said Jesse and he headed down to the river. The river was swollen out of its banks and was engulfing all the bushes and trees along the bank. There were logs and all kinds of debris rushing by.

Jesse caught movement out of the corner of his eye. He turned to look and there were two beavers up on the shore. He thought, *"Man, this must be some bad flood for beavers to leave the water in the middle of the day."* It was a terrible flood and it was a good thing that their house was back up on the hill. Jesse couldn't find the snake that he had hung in the tree. He really didn't set much store in that old saying anyway. *How could hanging a snake in a tree make it rain? It just didn't make any sense, but after this rain, maybe there is something to it.*

Jesse saw something else move at the edge of the water. It was a big ole snake and it was a rattlesnake. Then there was another snake coming out onto the bank. Looking out over the water, Jesse could see more snakes swimming in the current. The flood waters must be washing all the snakes out of the big swamp up–river. He had heard tales of this swamp, how it was covered with snakes and that no one would go into it. It must be true if that's where all these snakes were coming from.

Jesse had never seen so many snakes before and he had seen his share of them. This could develop into a bad situation. Everyone that lived along the river would be infested with poisonous snakes. *I'd better go warn everybody to be on the lookout,* he thought. Jesse took off running to his house first.

"Paw!" he hollered as he ran into the yard. "Paw, Paw, come here!"

"What's the matter Jesse?"

"The river's rising fast and there are more snakes than I ever saw. They must have washed down from the big swamp in the flood waters," Jesse said panting. "We got to warn everybody quick." Paw looked real concerned as he thought about the situation.

"They will probably just wash on down the river," Paw said.

"No, Paw. They're coming out on the banks and they're some bad snakes," Jesse said.

"Okay, you go down river and I'll go up."

"Maw!" Paw hollered into the house. "Stay in the house and keep the children inside away from the doors." Maw ran to the door.

"What in the world is going on?" she asked. "The river's flooding and it washed down a bunch of snakes from up river," Jesse said. "There are hundreds of them and they're coming out onto the bank."

"Snakes alive!" Maw shouted as she gathered the children inside and shut the door.

Paw went up river and Jesse went down, warning all the neighbors about the snakes. Some of them listened and some of them laughed at Jesse.

"We're being invaded by snakes," Jim Puckett called in to his wife. "Jesse said there's hundreds of them crawling out of the river and headed straight for us," he laughed.

"Now Jesse," Mrs. Puckett said, "you're not pulling our leg, are you? It's not very nice to be playing jokes on old people."

"No, ma'am," Jesse replied. "I saw them with my own two eyes. Ya'll keep a watch out for them. They're big and they're poison." Mr. and Mrs. Puckett were laughing as they went back inside.

It was almost dark and Jesse figured that he had better head back home. It would be real dangerous after dark. His Paw was doing the same thing and they met up back in their yard.

"Did you get to everybody?" Paw asked.

"Yes, sir, but I don't think they all believed me," said Jesse. "Well, they better," Paw said. "I saw a dozen or more down the road and back. All of them poisonous: copperheads, cottonmouths, and rattlesnakes."

"We had better get back inside," Paw said. With that, they went inside and closed all the doors and windows, made sure that there were no holes left open that a snake could come in and went to bed with their minds running wild with ideas about how to handle the snake problem.

Everyone was up at daylight. There was too much excitement for sleeping late. Jesse went to the window to check things out and there were two big rattlesnakes coiled on the porch. "Paw, look at this," Jesse said. Paw came over to the window and saw the two snakes and his skin began to crawl. Paw never had cared too much for snakes and wasn't going to start now.

Maw looked out the window and screamed, "Snakes alive!" Paw had got the shotgun down and was going to shoot them right where they lay.

"Don't shoot the porch, Paw. I'll get them off and on the ground and then you can shoot."

"Don't go out there," Maw pleaded, but Jesse knew what he had to do. He opened the door and both of the snakes started rattling. Jesse took a stick and threw the snakes on the ground and they had no sooner hit the ground when Paw shot them.

"Paw, I've got to go help the neighbors out before someone gets bitten," Jesse said.

"Okay, son, I'll clean up around here. You watch yourself," said Paw.

Jesse took a hoe from the barn and headed down river. He could hear Paw's shotgun going off in the distance and knew that there wouldn't be any snakes there when he returned.

He came to the Jones' farm first. They hadn't come outside yet, but were standing at the window, looking at a porch full of snakes. Jesse started chopping the snakes with the hoe and cleared them all off of the porch. Mr. Jones came out and thanked Jesse.

"Boy, I'm sure glad to see you. I ain't never seen snakes like this. They're everywhere."

"I've got to go to the next farm and help them Mr. Jones. If you'll get your shotgun and clean up here, I'll stop by on my way back to check on you," said Jesse.

"I'll sure do that," said Mr. Jones as he ran back into the house to get his gun.

Heading down the road to the next farm, Jesse could hear Mr. Jones shooting. He could also hear his Paw's gun going off in the distance. *There will be a bunch of dead snakes to clean up,* he thought.

The next farm was the Wilkens' and he could hear screaming up ahead. He took off running and could hear a commotion coming from inside. He ran up on the porch and there were two dead snakes and four live ones. Jesse quickly dispatched the live ones and threw them off of the porch. Mr. Wilkens was lying on the floor holding his leg. Mrs. Wilkens was going hysterical and running around in the house.

"Jesse, I tried to kill them, but one got me from behind."

"What kind was it?" asked Jesse.

"Copperhead," Mr. Wilkens said. His leg was already starting to swell.

"That's better than a cottonmouth or rattlesnake," Jesse said. "Copperheads don't have as strong of venom." Jesse tied a piece of rope around Mr. Wilkens' leg and told him to lay still and loosen the rope every ten minutes.

"You think you need to cut it and suck the poison out?" Mr. Wilkens asked.

"No, not with a copperhead bite. Just lay as still as you can. You don't want to get your heart rate up and pump the venom all over your body," Jesse said. "I'll get the Doc to come by as soon as I can. Mrs. Wilkens, keep him plenty of water to drink and try to calm down. He'll be okay. This won't kill him."

Jesse took off to the Pucket's farm as fast as he could run. When he got there, the door was wide open and snakes were everywhere. He killed the ones on the porch and went in the door. Mr. and Mrs. Pucket were lying on the floor with snakes all around them. They had been bitten nine or ten times each and these weren't copperheads lying around them. He was too late. Mr. and Mrs. Pucket were both dead.

An awful feeling ran through his veins, almost making him sick. But he didn't have time for this feeling. He had to walk away from death and try to help someone else.

All day, Jesse helped everyone he could and killed an unknown number of snakes. It must have been in the hundreds. The shotgun blast had subsided to one every now and then. He met up with his Paw, Mr. Jones, and some other men on his way back home.

"Paw, Mr. and Mrs. Pucket didn't make it. I tried to get to them, but I was too late." Jesse was feeling mighty bad about Mr. and Mrs. Pucket, but they wouldn't listen to him.

"I know, son, we went by there. They must have walked right out on top of them. We got the Doc over to Mr. Wilkens and he's going to be okay," said Paw, sensing the helpless feeling that Jesse had about Mr. and Mrs. Pucket. "You know, if you hadn't warned everybody, there would be a lot more people dead. You did all you could do. Sometimes, no matter how hard you try, you can't prevent bad things from happening. All you can do is your best and go on."

Paw's words helped him a little bit as they always did. His Paw was a wise man and Jesse knew it. But he still had an empty feeling about Mr. and Mrs. Puckett lying there on the floor of their own house with those snakes all around them.

The days passed and the snake problem slowly went away. Jesse had been on a mission, one long snake hunt and didn't slack off until they were all gone.

Things slowly got back to normal around the river. Mr. and Mrs. Pucket were missed. Mr. Wilkens couldn't thank Jesse enough. It was safe to go fishing and swimming once again.

Times were good and things were looking up for Jesse. He had been offered a job catching snakes on some island in the Pacific Ocean and was thinking about taking the job, but hadn't told Maw yet. Knowing that this wouldn't set very well with her, he hesitated, but knew deep down that he should go. He might save someone's life. He might not be too late, as he was with Mr. and Mrs. Pucket.

So he decided to tell her one night after supper. Maw was rocking Jean to sleep, in her old rocking chair when Jesse told her about his plans. She looked at him and then back down at Jean as she rocked her and said, "Snakes Alive, Jesse, Snakes Alive."

The moral of this story is …
Fear lingers and grows if left unchecked.

Gold Cave

Back in the days of the early Spanish explorers, somewhere in the southern United States, somewhere in Central Alabama, somewhere on the Coosa River, somewhere in the back of a cave in a huge chest was four hundred pounds of gold coins. Well, that's the way legend has it at least.

One of the early Spanish explorers came up the river from the Gulf of Mexico, and in his ship was a treasure chest full of gold coins. At some point during his journey up the river, he was attacked by Creek Indians. Many of his men were killed and his ship was left disabled. The explorer decided that he should hide his gold until the ship was repaired.

During his search to find a place, he stumbled upon a cave and it turned out to be the perfect place to hide his treasure. He also left his bride to be, Penelope Wentworth, with the gold and told her that he would return to get her. With Penelope and the treasure safely hidden, he began repairing the ship. But word had gotten out about his gold and a band of renegades had followed him. They took the ship by surprise and killed everyone on it except the explorer himself. They tortured him for three days trying to get him to tell where the gold was. The night air was filled with his awful screams as they echoed down the river with an eerie and frightful sound. They say that the Indians nearby even left the river because of the evil spirits.

Unable to make the explorer talk, the renegades cut off his head and threw his body into the river. As his lifeblood drained into the water, it is said that it settled on a rock right in front of the cave, on the riverbank. Legend has it that one man once found the rock and the cave, but was never seen again. So, the gold still lies untouched in the cave.

About three hundred years later, a young man decided that he was going to find out if the legend was true or just a myth. His name was Jordan Wheeler; he was six foot– two inches tall, 190 pounds, with light brown hair and green eyes. A handsome young man, who walked and moved with the ease of a cat. Jordan did a lot of reading and listened to the old–timers. He respected them very much and showed it by listening to everything they said. But he had learned not to be too gullible. You have to watch those old rascals; they'll feed you a line, hook you, and reel you all the way in and laugh about it for hours.

One day, Jordan heard them talking about Gold Cave. This story really sparked an interest in him.

"Ya'll telling me that gold is in a cave on the banks of the Coosa River?" he asked.

"Sure is," said Slim Johnson, who was the chief bull–crapper and a very smart man. "Of course, it's under water now because they backed the river up when they built the dam."

"What part of the river?" Jordan asked.

"Well, it's hard to say, but I think it is somewhere in between Otter Cove and Blue Creek."

"Thanks, Slim. I am going to find out if this legend is true or not."

"Watch yourself, boy. That current is mighty strong right there," Slim said.

They said goodbye and the old–timers laughed and said, "That Jordan Wheeler will believe anything."

Slim said, "Maybe, but if that gold is really out there, he'll find it."

Jordan couldn't quit thinking about Gold Cave; he just couldn't get it off his mind. Even when he picked up his girlfriend, Jill, she knew that he was preoccupied with something.

"Jordan, what's bothering you? You're not paying me any attention, and I'm even wearing your favorite dress."

"Oh, I'm sorry," Jordan said. "I just can't stop thinking about what the old–timers were talking about today. There's a cave on the riverbank with four hundred pounds of gold coins that have been there for three hundred years." Jill shot out at Jordan like a snake striking a rat.

"You've been listening to them again? Do you not remember what happened the last time? Everyone in town was laughing at you, a grown man trying to catch a bear with a lollipop. Just get close enough to the bear, hold the lollipop out, and when the bear gets it in his mouth, you just lead him around like a puppy. That bear almost killed you. They're setting you up for the fall, just so they can get a laugh and you're just dumb enough to fall for it again."

"But Honey, this time it's different," Jordan said.

"Don't 'honey' me, Jordan Wheeler. You pay more attention to those old codgers than you do to me. When you come back to your senses, you give me a call, but I'm not going to sit here and play second fiddle to some idiotic brain wave you just happened to have. Goodbye!" screamed Jill and stomped out of the diner.

Jordan just put his head in his hands and moaned. Slim Johnson happened to be close enough to hear what was going on. He strolled over to Jordan, put his hand on his shoulder, and said, "Cheer up, Jordan, it will get better, but I don't think you're going to get any sugar tonight."

Jordan woke up the next morning and already had his plan worked out. All he had to do was dive down in the river, find a red rock or cave entrance, go into the cave, find the gold, and just walk or swim out. Plus, when he found that gold,

Jill would be all lovey–dovey. Simple? Yes. Likely to happen? No, but being the optimist that he was, he would give it a shot.

Down at the river, Jordan got into his boat and started upriver, planning to work his way down with the current. He tied his boat up to the bank, got his mask and swim fins on, and hit the water.

About four hours later with no luck at all, Jordan was getting water logged. He looked at his watch and said, "Thirty minutes more and I'm heading home." He dove again. Jordan could hold his breath for about two minutes if he didn't exert himself. This was something that he was very proud of; no one around could stay under water as long as him. Most people thought that he was part fish.

Working his way down the river bank, he swam up to a large red rock. *This must be it*, he thought. The red rock was very strange looking; it looked like fresh blood and Jordan touched it. It was real blood and it came off on his hand. *This is a little spooky,* he thought, and headed back up to get some air. When he surfaced, he found a landmark on the bank so that he wouldn't lose his place. It was a large pine tree with an eagle's nest in it.

Jordan caught his breath and went back down. Now the rock seemed to be glowing and the blood was fresher than before. There was a small hole above the rock, but it wasn't large enough to get into. But, this must be the cave entrance. Jordan pulled at the rocks and mud and it just fell away making a large hole. Back up for air, he got his light out of the boat and headed back down. The hole went down on an angle for twenty feet and then turned up.

After surveying the situation, he decided to get more air and swim into the hole, even though it would be a little scary. Down again with his lungs full of air, he didn't hesitate, right into the hole and up the turn. There was a small hole there and it looked like there might be air on the other side. *No turning back now,* he thought.

The entrance was very tight, but he thought that he could get through it. All of the sudden a rock came loose and wedged Jordan in the hole. He pushed and pulled, but couldn't get free. Reaching up as far as he could, his hand came out of the water, there was air up there, but it had already been two minutes and his air was gone. Jordan's life flashed before his eyes, and he thought, *This is it. I should have gotten help.* That was the last thing he thought. His lights were going out and his air was gone.

Back in town that night, Jill was looking for Jordan without any luck. She ran into Slim Johnson.

"Have you seen Jordan? I can't find him anywhere."

Slim answered, "No, I haven't. He was heading down to the river this morning."

"Yeah, I bet he was looking for that gold that some idiot told him about. You wouldn't know anything about that would you, Slim?" she asked.

"Well, he might have overheard us talking yesterday," Slim said.

"I'm sure he did," Jill flared. "He's so foolish, he'll end up hanging out with the rest of ya'll fools. I don't ever want to see him again." With that, Jill stomped off with smoke coming out of her ears.

Slim got a little worried then, but thought, *Jordan had been out many a night fishing and hunting. If he's not back in the morning, I'll go find him.* Slim went home and went to bed, but he didn't sleep much. He had a bad feeling about this, but Jordan was a grown man and nobody told him what he could or couldn't do—except, maybe Jill.

The next morning, Slim went down to the river, but Jordan's boat wasn't there. "I'd better go looking for him," he said to himself. Slim headed up river in his boat. He knew where to go. Otter Cove is where he told Jordan to look for the gold.

Slim spotted Jordan's boat tied to the bank by a tall pine tree. He pulled up alongside it, but there was no sign of Jordan—there was no sign of anything. Slim walked the banks and up over the hill, but no sign. Then it hit him; he must have gone into the water. Slim felt sick deep down inside. If Jordan had drowned, it would be his fault. Slim lit out back to town to get some help. The whole time he was thinking that he had gotten Jordan killed by running his mouth about that gold.

There were ten boats with drags searching for Jordan. They dragged up the river, down the river, and across the river, but nothing turned up. After a week of searching, the search was called off. Everyone figured that Jordan had drowned and the strong current had washed him down under something. They would never find him.

It was a sad day when they had Jordan Wheeler's funeral. There was no body to bury; they just had a service for him. No one could really believe that he had drowned, because he was the best swimmer in the county. Slim and Jill took it the hardest, as each blamed themselves. Jill, because she had gotten mad and said she never wanted to see him again. Slim, because he had filled his head with that stupid Gold Cave story. Things just weren't the same around town anymore. Everyone was sad; the dogs didn't even bark. Jordan Wheeler dead—it seemed impossible.

Jordan's eyes opened and he gasped for air, and it was there. He wasn't drowning; he wasn't even in the water. He was in the cave and there was a warm glow from a fire. *How did I get here, I was stuck in the hole and passed out.* He thought as he looked around at the damp rock walls, glistening from the fire light.

As he scanned his surrounding, his eyes fixed on a beautiful young lady, wearing a full length bright green dress that looked as though it had come out of a history book. She had long dark hair, a beautiful face and eyes that looked like they were unreal. She looked very normal except for the eyes, which confused Jordan even more. He had no idea what was going on, but he was alive.

Jordan started to rise and she saw that he was awake.

"You're finally awake, my love," she said with delight.

"How did I get here? Did you drag me out of the water?" Jordan asked.

"I have waited for you, my love, and finally you have come," She said with a smile.

Jordan could sense that something was not on the up and up. The girl acted as if she knew him, but he had never seen her before.

"What's your name?" Jordan asked.

"You know. I am Penelope Wentworth and we are to be married," she said and ran to him and kissed him. Jordan started to resist, thinking about Jill, but the pleasure he felt from Penelope's lips pressed against his was beyond resistance and he kissed her back with much passion. His mind lost in the moment, unaware that his life force was being drained from his body and the danger that he was in. His thoughts went blank as he slipped into the darkness.

Something wet was dripping on Jordan's face and he awoke to an empty cave. Water was dripping from the cave ceiling and the fire was still burning, but Penelope was not there. Jordan got up, still weak from the kiss, and looked around the cave. There it was, the chest, sitting in the corner of the cave. The chest looked so old. Could it be full of gold? Jordan opened the chest and it almost blinded him. It was full of shiny gold coins. So, the legend was true, but what about the girl and where was she?

Penelope suddenly appeared out of nowhere, frowning slightly.

"Sometimes I think you love that gold more than you do me. Come to me, my love," she said. She was so beautiful that Jordan couldn't resist. It was like she had a spell on him. She kissed him long and hard; he was staggered on his feet. She was draining his senses.

"I will return, my love, and we will die together. We will be together forever," she said as she turned and walked through the cave wall.

Jordan couldn't believe what he was seeing. She was a ghost and she wanted him to die so that they could be together. *If she keeps kissing me like that, I will be dead,* he thought. Jordan knew that he had to go and he had to go fast. *But what about the gold? But what about dying down here in this cave with a beautiful ghost?*

Jordan wanted the gold, but knew it would be impossible to get out with it. So, he grabbed a handful of coins and stuffed them into his pant pocket. He started down toward the entrance just as Penelope came back through the wall.

"You can't leave me again," she said and cut him off from the cave entrance. "Kiss me, my love," she said and reached for him. Jordan ducked the love hold and grabbed her dress to throw her aside, but the dress had dry rotted from three hundred years of wear. It fell to pieces in Jordan's hands and he fell into a trance at the sight of Penelope standing there totally naked.

"Kiss me my love!" she begged in desperation and Jordan took a step toward her, but then abruptly stopped. Penelope's face suddenly started to wrinkle, her hair became frizzy and gray and her skin was shriveling up over her bones. The beautiful Penelope had turned into a living mummy.

Jordan, snapped out of his trance by this gruesome transformation, was no longer interested in Penelope's kiss. He started backing slowly toward the water to make his escape, but Penelope wasn't willing to let him go.

She reached for him and screamed, "Come to me, my love!" Jordan made his move and dove into the water with Penelope grabbing him by the leg as he plunged in. As soon as her hand touched the water, she relinquished her hold and ushered a spine tingling scream of anguish.

She was an eternal captive to the cave and could never go into the water.

Jordan swam down into the hole that he had been stuck in when he had first found the cave. The hole was tight, but this time he managed to push through with sheer determination and no desire to return to Penelope.

When Jordan reached the surface, it was pitch black, the middle of the night, but what night he did not know. He climbed up onto the bank and could hear Penelope screaming.

"I'm not staying here until daylight," he said. With that he gathered his bearings from the stars and started swimming. He might drown, but he wasn't going to stay on the same side of the river with Penelope.

Three hours later, the sun was starting to rise and Slim Johnson was on his way to the dock. Ever since the funeral, Slim would go down to the river at daylight. Maybe he thought that he would see Jordan pulling up in his boat. But the boat was there and it was always empty.

Slim started to turn back to town, when he caught a glimpse of something moving in the water and it was swimming. *Must be a deer,* he thought. But it wasn't. *What was somebody doing swimming at this time of morning?* Slim stared at the swimmer in disbelief. "I must be going crazy," Slim said.

Jordan saw Slim standing on the dock and let out a whoop that Slim would know. Slim almost fell off of the dock.

"Jordan, is that you, Jordan?"

Jordan called back, "Well, I ain't no mermaid! Now help me out. I'm so water logged, I'm about to sink." Slim grabbed Jordan and gave him a bear hug that almost broke his back.

"Slim, hold on, I missed you too, but you're killing me," Jordan wheezed.

"Where have you been Jordan? You've been gone three weeks," Slim said.

"I've been in Gold Cave, but I was only there one day."

"You've been gone longer than that. We had your funeral two weeks ago," Slim said, as he took a step back and looked at Jordan with unbelieving eyes. He had lost at least thirty pounds, had a grizzled beard, gaunt face and hollow eyes.

"What happened to you? Where have you been? We looked everywhere for you!"

"I've just been gone one day Slim and I found Gold Cave," Jordan replied with a smile.

"You've been gone three weeks!" Slim paused to catch his breath. "We had your funeral last week. I thought that you had drowned and it was my fault for telling you about that cave..."

As they walked back to town, Jordan explained what had happened. Slim thought that Jordan had lost his mind.

"Let's go see Doc Harper. He can figure out what's wrong with you," Slim said.

"I'm telling you the truth, Slim. I don't need to go see Doc Harper. I just need some grub; I'm starving to death."

They went into Rob's Diner and everyone went crazy.

"Jordan's alive, Jordan's alive!" they called and ran through town telling everyone. Jill heard all of the commotion outside and went to the door to see what was going on. *Jordan's alive? Could it be possible?* She ran right out of her shoes, she was moving so fast.

"Jordan's alive; he's at Rob's Diner," someone called out and Jill left a smoke trail down the dusty road.

Jordan was trying to explain to everyone what had happened, but then thought better. It might not be a good idea to tell anyone about Gold Cave. Someone could get killed down there. Just then Jill busted through the door.

When she saw Jordan, she ran to him and gave him a big kiss right on the smacker. *Now that's some good sugar,* he thought as he held her tightly for a long moment and realized how much that he really cared for her. His encounter with Penelope had been an awakening, if nothing else and he would forevermore have a different perspective on life. Jill couldn't believe that he was here alive. Neither could anyone else, but after awhile, things settled down some.

Jordan, Jill, and Slim were sitting at a table alone.

"Now I want to know what happened, Jordan Wheeler," Jill said. So he went over the whole story. Jill and Slim looked at each other, knowing that something was wrong with Jordan's brain.

"Look, I'm telling you the truth and I've got proof."

"Yeah, show us the proof," Slim scoffed. Jordan looked around to make sure no one else was looking and pulled two gold coins out of his pocket. He handed one to Jill and one to Slim. They looked at each other again. Jordan was telling the truth.

"Now, do you believe me?" Jordan asked. They both nodded yes and Jordan said,

"Good, now can a starving man get something to eat around here?"

Slim jumped up and hollered, "Rob, bring out your biggest steak, medium rare, and make it snappy!"

Meanwhile, Jill had laid a kiss on Jordan that wouldn't quit. Slim just sat back and smiled, "I can't wait to go to that cave and get the rest of that gold."

Jordan smiled back and said, "I ain't going back. I have all of the sugar I need right here."

The moral of this story is…
Don't let the luster of gold blind you
from the fortune you hold.

Chasing Beavers

Back in the days before technology took its grip on the people of the world, people used their imagination and whatever else was there to amuse themselves. It really didn't take much; a rock to throw, a stick to draw in the dirt with or a vine to swing on. Simple, yes, but a very ample antidote for boredom.

Just thinking about these simple pleasures brings back memories of yesteryear. Frog gigging, snake hunting, catching tadpoles, and a vast number of other activities that kept us busy, after all of the chores were done, of course. One of my favorite past times was something most people would think was very unusual indeed and a lot of people thought that it was crazy.

Chasing Beavers. Yep, that's what I said. No mistake. Chasing Beavers. This past time is maybe a little more than simple, but what fun we had. I say we, because chasing beavers is fun for the whole family. Maw, Paw, brothers and sisters, can all partake in this fascinating event. All that was needed was a lake or river, some type of boat, and of course, a beaver.

Our family lived on the west side of the Coosa River. We had a canoe and a couple of paddles, and boy, did we have beavers. We happened up on the idea of chasing beavers quite by accident as I was awakened one morning by Maw's screams.

"Get away from my plum tree, you varmint. Logan, get up and catch that beaver. He's chewed down my plum tree!"

Maw was pretty distraught, and jumping out of the bed, I ran to the door in time to see the beaver headed for the river, dragging Maw's plum tree behind. I ran after him, not even taking time to put on my shoes, but it was too late. The beaver was in the water, headed home with his breakfast. I jumped into the canoe and took off. The chase was on and it didn't take long for me to catch up with him because he couldn't swim very fast dragging the plum tree.

When I did catch up to him, I guess it made him a little nervous. He dropped the plum tree and popped his tail on the water as he dove underneath the surface. I grabbed the tree and put it in the boat. I really don't know why; it certainly wasn't any good now. I guess it was just because it was Maw's plum tree. Maybe she would stick it back down in the ground and try to root it.

The beaver came back up about fifty feet away and I decided quickly to chase him. *I'll teach you a lesson,* I thought. He popped his tail again and disappeared under the water. It's pretty neat watching a beaver pop his tail, which is really a signal that alerts the other beavers of danger.

I paddled really fast to close the distance on him and up he came, a little closer than before. He was a smart beaver, always changing directions on me. This went on for thirty minutes or more and I began to catch on to his pattern of direction. The next time he popped his tail and went under, I changed my direction, guessing in which direction he would go.

This time, my move was right on target. The beaver came up right beside the canoe and when he saw how close he was, it scared him to death. He popped his tail so hard and fast that it splashed water all over me. I just laughed and stopped paddling. I was thinking, *Hey, this is fun, even more fun than chasing a chicken*. He stayed under a long time, coming up about fifty yards away. I waved and said, "So long old boy."

Well that's how we got started chasing beavers. There for a while we were chasing beavers two or three times a week. My brothers, sisters, Paw and even Maw went with me one day. That's a chase I will always remember. It was so funny watching Maw stare down those beavers, always asking, "Are you the one that cut down my plum tree?" That was a trip to remember until my dying days.

We were having so much fun that it took awhile for us to realize that the beavers were having fun, too. Some evenings there would be three or four of them swimming around in front of the boat landing, waiting on us to come and play. We would take off after one of them and the others would flank us on both sides. When the one out front would pop his tail, the others would follow suit. Always changing directions every time the beavers went under, trying to outsmart them and when we did it just right, there was a great sense of accomplishment.

Doing it right was not easy to do. The idea was to change directions quickly and stop paddling because they can hear that and home in on your location. Then, if you've made the right move and the beaver comes up close to you, but facing away from you and doesn't even know that you are behind him. Then holler, "Got ya!" real loud. It will scare the fur off of him. You'll laugh like crazy and I'm sure that it is very exhilarating to the beaver, because after they recuperate, they always come back for more.

Word got around to all of our kinfolk and neighbors about how much fun we were having and our home got to be a busy place. Maw told me, "Son, we're going to have to start charging admission for all these beaver chasers. I don't know if I can feed them all." After that I fixed up one of our old feed houses and turned it into a snack shack. I had to do something because Maw wouldn't have anyone going hungry. She would cook our last bean and then I would be hungry!

The Snack Shack turned out pretty nice. I stocked it with some very good canned goods like sardines, potted meat, and of course, Beanie Weenies. We also had some candy bars, crackers, and hot Coca–Colas. There were plenty of snacks to keep all of the beaver chasers from starving.

As word spread around, everyone wanted in on the action. One day a newspaper reporter came out and did an article on chasing beavers. This was very gratifying, but turned out to be the beginning of the end for our little operation. Everything was moving so fast, that it took hold of us like a whirlwind and we couldn't get loose.

The next thing that I knew, one of those animal rights people showed up, claiming that we were causing the beavers mental anguish. But, Sheriff Smith sent her on her way, telling her that the beavers were living longer and more healthy lives because of the aerobic exercise they were getting from being chased, which made sense to me, but anyhow, she loaded up her protest sign and left.

Then the Health Department inspector showed up and wanted to see the bathroom and kitchen facilities. I opened the door to the Snack Shack and pointed out toward the woods to show him the restroom. After a short inspection, there was no more Snack Shack. The inspector had shut me down.

I was sitting on a stump, wondering what I was going to do now. No snacks for the chasers. We would all be out of vittles in a week at the house. There were cars and trucks parked all over the farm. We had borrowed extra boats for all the visitors and all my brothers and cousins were acting as guides. Things had gotten out of control.

While I sat there pondering the situation, I heard screaming coming from the river. I couldn't make out what was going on with all the laughing, tail popping, and screaming. So I took off down there and saw a woman standing up in the canoe, screaming, with a baby in her arms. The number one rule in a canoe is never stand up. She had seen a snake in the water and Cousin Jim was doing all he could do to calm her and keep the canoe from turning over, but it happened. I was standing there watching as the canoe flipped over and the baby shot out of the screaming woman's arms. I glanced around for another boat to get in, but they were all gone.

There was no time to spare. I stripped down to my underwear and dove in. Swimming as fast as Tarzan in those old movies when a forty foot crocodile was after him, I was to the boat in a flash. Jim had a hold of the woman and the canoe. That was all he could handle because the woman had really lost it when she lost her grip on her baby.

With no sign of the child on the surface, I dove under and searched for the child, but couldn't see him in the dingy water. I tried and tried, but no baby. Some more boats had pulled up around us and it seemed as if all was lost. It grew so quiet; the only sounds that could be heard were the mournful sobs of the young mother.

All of the sudden, the beavers started popping their tails like crazy. Someone hollered, "There's the baby!" This is almost unbelievable, but everyone there saw it. The beavers had found the baby. The old beaver was under the baby, holding him up on the surface on his back and three more beavers circling, while popping their tails.

I swam over to them and retrieved the young child and the beavers calmly hung around until the mother and child were safely in a boat. I turned and looked the old beaver right in the eyes, and that was eye level because I was still in the water. The beaver looked back at me and I swear that he knew exactly what he was doing. The beaver had sensed the dangerous situation and had come to the rescue. As I looked him in his dark eyes, just as I was about to turn and swim back to the shore, he winked—the old rascal winked at me! Then he calmly slid under the water.

Well, the beaver chasing operation was over. All the people were gone, the borrowed boats returned, and the Snack Shack was restocked with animal feed. Things had returned to normal around home again and we were all glad of it, too. Maw had planted a new plum tree and I put a wire around it to discourage our hungry friends. I still went beaver chasing every now and then, but kept a low profile about it. The beavers seemed to be very happy when I did chase them, especially the old beaver. He was still pretty slick; sometimes I won and sometimes he did.

Forty years later, I still go beaver chasing every now and then with my family and friends. It's still fun and it still brings back memories of the fun we had years ago. A lot of things have changed, but the beavers still seem to be the same. Like timeless creatures that never change. Even though I'm a little slower now and Maw's plum tree never did survive, the fun's still out there. All it takes is a little imagination to go along with something that is already there.

The moral of this story is…
Simple pleasures make happy fellers.

Holy Possum

"Get up boys, time to get ready for church," Maw hollered. Maw started every Sunday morning the same way, rousing all six of her children out of bed and into the kitchen for breakfast.

"Jim, Jim, where are you? Has anybody seen Jim?" Maw asked as she stomped out on the porch looking for Paw. "Jim Johnson, I know you can hear me! It's time for church." But Paw didn't answer. Maw stormed back inside mumbling something about a heathen.

All of us kids were at the table munching down on a good Sunday morning breakfast. Cat-head biscuits (biscuits as big as the head of a cat) salt pork, grits, eggs and blackberry jelly. Maw really knew how to cook and we weren't late for the table very often.

Meanwhile, Paw had slipped out the back. He heard Maw calling him, but kept on paddling, because he was going fishing; Paw loved to fish on Sunday morning and he really didn't like listening to Reverend Jones. He said that Reverend Jones went on and on so long that it would put a soul to sleep, except that Reverend Jones' whiney voice was so irritating that you couldn't sleep.

Paw talked to the Lord in his own way and I know this to be a fact, because every time he caught a fish, he would say, "Thank you, Lord," and put it on the stringer.

Back at the house, Maw had fed us all and was making sure that we were all dressed properly. With this all done, she lined us all up and made any last minute adjustments if necessary. Then she would look at us and throw her hands up in the air and shout, "Thank you, Lord Jesus for these fine children and look after my heathen husband wherever he is. Amen."

We all knew to start walking as soon as she said, "Amen," so we headed off down the dirt road toward Chissom Creek Baptist Church. It was about a two mile walk and we made it every Sunday, unless there was lightning. Maw didn't like lightning. She said it was the Lord's sword striking down evil spirits and that we didn't need to be out on the battlefield, less we might be mistakenly struck down. She said that the Lord was getting pretty old and she didn't know how good his eyesight was anymore.

We arrived about thirty minutes early, as always, and we were in fairly good shape. Little Bob had jumped in a mud hole and had mud all over him, but it really didn't matter because I don't think anyone at church had ever seen Bob without mud on him somewhere. John had a knot on his head where Will had hit him with a rock and Will had whelps on his legs where Maw had switched him. All in all, it was one of our more successful walks to church.

We walked into the churchyard and Maw was speaking to everyone about anything new that had happened in the community that week. The older men were gathered up on the far end of the yard exchanging cuts off of assorted plugs of tobacco. That's where I headed, hoping that Mr. Watson would give me a cut of his Brown's Mule without Maw finding out.

Reverend Jones walked up to Maw and said, "Good morning, Mrs. Johnson, and how are you doing on this fine morning?"

"Very well, Reverend Jones. I'm just grateful that the Lord has given us another day."

"That's the spirit Sister!" Reverend Jones smiled. "And where is Mr. Johnson today?"

Maw's face drew on a concerned look, "Reverend, I don't know what I am going to do with Jim. He slipped out of the house this morning while I was cooking breakfast. He's probably down on the river fishing."

"Maybe I should go and talk with him next week," Reverend Jones offered.

"Oh, no," said Maw. "The last time you talked to him, he started slipping out on Saturday and didn't come home until Monday. At least now he's home on Saturday." Reverend Jones frowned a little and said, "Everyone come inside now; it's time for the service to get started."

The women and children started in first as the old men lingered while they spit their tobacco out and wiped their faces as best they could. Maw guided us to our regular pew and lined us all up before we could sit down. She always wanted the three youngest on her right because she was right handed and could twist an ear if necessary. The three oldest were on her left and we knew that if we cut up, we would get cut down later.

Reverend Jones made the usual announcements and started on the prayer list. When he got to the end of the list he said, "And we need to say a special prayer for Jim Johnson, that he might see the light and come to church on Sunday morning."

John spoke up and said, "We can't even see the church from our house preacher, much less a light in the window."

All the men and children busted out laughing and the women cut their eyes at John and frowned while Maw was putting a twist on John's ear to silence him. Reverend Jones interrupted, "Let's have reverence in the Lord's House. That's not the kind of light I was talking about." The laughter stopped and everyone's attention was on the preacher.

It kind of caught him off guard and he had to explain himself, "It's the light from the Lord." We were all thinking about lightning and sat there with bewildered looks on our faces as Reverend Jones continued, "The light of the Lord. You know, from heaven." He paused, at a loss for words. "Brother Mims, would you come up and lead us in a song?"

Brother Mims was a happy, cheerful man in his fifties that everyone liked. He hopped up and grabbed a hymnal and we were off and singing.

We all loved to sing and it made Maw proud to see us all join in. We were probably the loudest pew in the whole church.

Brother Mims led us in three songs and then he said, "Let's sing *Heavenly Sunlight*," which was my favorite and he knew it. He asked me to come up and help with the song and I did. That song set the tone for Reverend Jones. The whole congregation was ready to worship the Lord.

Reverend Jones started preaching and he was really letting the hammer down. Over half of the congregation had their feet pulled back under the pews because he was stepping on their toes.

Mrs. Davis was feeling guilty because she had been gossiping and vowed never to gossip again; which lasted until church services were over and she found someone to talk to. John Moore felt ashamed because he had been looking at Chet Walker's wife. The list went on and on as Reverend Jones was on one of his *Tell it all brother* sermons.

Allan Morris jumped up and confessed, "Lord, forgive me. I haven't been as good of a husband as I should have."

"Tell it all brother!" Reverend Jones responded with much enthusiasm.

"Lord, forgive me. I received more change than I should have at the grocery store and I kept it."

"Tell it all brother!"

"Lord forgive me. I stole one of Bob Rush's goats and sold it back to him yesterday." The whole congregation stood up and looked at Allan as Reverend Jones broke the silence saying, "I don't believe that I would have told that brother," with a very concerned look on his face.

Meanwhile Bob Rush had started out of his pew with a message for Allan, who wasn't hanging around to receive it. He ran out of the front doors of the church with Bob right on his heels. Reverend Jones finally controlled the situation, as Allan and Bob were conducting their business outside, he continued his sermon.

Well, Reverend Jones went on and on and on. I was starting to get hungry and little Bob was fidgeting around like he had ants in his pants. I liked coming to church and the singing. I even liked the first forty–five minutes of the preacher's sermon, but the other hour was hard to take.

Mrs. Wilson was sweating and had her hand fan going wide open when something wet touched her leg. She looked down and there was a possum bearing his big teeth and slobbering on her leg. She jumped up on the pew with a loud, "Lord, help me!" Then other people started standing up and shouting, "Yes, Lord help her!"

There was a whole lot of repenting going on and that possum had started it all. About that time, that possum ran across the aisle and I saw him. I guess it had been hiding under one of the pews and had took all he could take of Reverend Jones' sermon and was trying to get out of church before he went crazy.

I jumped up and headed up the aisle to catch the possum and Reverend Jones shouted, "Come on down, my son." I was headed up that aisle pretty fast and took a hard right as Reverend Jones was coming down to meet me.

I caught up with the possum at the edge of the first pew, (which I was always curious about, because nobody ever seemed to sit there). As I grabbed the possum by the tail and snatched him up, Reverend Jones was coming to meet me with open arms. When I turned around with that possum bearing those big teeth, Reverend Jones fell out, flat of his back.

Mrs. Wilson, seeing what had happened to the preacher, passed out cold and she was still standing on the pew. She fell like a wet rag, right in George Lucas' lap. When Mrs. Lucas, who had been praising the Lord with her hands up in the air and her eyes shut, opened her eyes and saw Mrs. Wilson in her husband's lap, well, it wasn't a pretty sight. She picked up a hymnal and was beating poor George over the head with it.

It sure was a sight; women screaming and running out of the church doors. Most of the men were laughing their heads off, while some of them were screaming and headed out the doors with the women. "It's just an old possum!" I hollered, but that didn't seem to calm anyone down.

Well, I was standing there in church holding that possum and I figured that I had better get him out of there, so I headed out the front doors with him. As soon as I got out the doors, everyone that had run outside screaming took off running and screaming again.

I stood there grinning like the possum that I was holding at such a sight. All the boys gathered around me to get a good look at the possum. "Look there, that possum has got a notch in his ear," one of the boys said. I looked down and sure enough, there was a notch in his right ear and I knew that notch.

I had been possum hunting with Paw many times and if he caught one that he didn't want to keep, he would notch his ear. A lot of the old timers did that so they would know if they ever caught that particular possum again. Well, that notch was Paw's notch, but I didn't say anything. Paw was in enough trouble as it was.

Reverend Jones and Mrs. Wilson finally came to and realized that it wasn't one of Satan's demons, but just an old possum. Some of the congregation was straightening up the mess in the church, while I was about to release the scared possum at the edge of the woods. Mr. Watson walked up to me right before I turned the possum loose. "I sure would like to have that possum. I'll trade you a plug of Brown's Mule for him."

That was a deal that I couldn't afford to turn down. So I took the plug of tobacco and Mr. Watson headed home with his possum. Meanwhile, Maw had rounded all her children up and we headed home. All the way home, Maw kept saying over and over, "I wonder how that possum got into the church. It just don't make sense."

When we got home, Paw was sitting on the porch and Maw was so bent out of shape about that possum disrupting the service that she didn't even ask Paw where he had been. She went on and on about the whole ordeal and Paw would say, "No, you don't say," and try to look real serious, but I could see the twinkle in his eyes.

Maw finally quit ranting about the possum and how Reverend Jones had fell out cold and went into the house to start supper. With Maw inside, Paw couldn't hold it anymore. He just busted out belly laughing so hard that I started laughing, too.

Paw grinned and his eyes sparkled all evening long and I knew what he had done. Paw had gone down to the church on Saturday night and put that possum in the church. I guess it all worked out just as he had planned it, too.

I just couldn't stand it anymore and asked, "Paw, how do you think that possum got into the church?"

Paw rubbed his chin for a moment and said, "Well, a possum is always looking for something," then paused and said, "I guess he was just looking for the Lord. He must have been a holy possum." We laughed and went inside for supper. This had been a Sunday to remember.

The moral of this story is ...
A creature as simply as a possum,
can sometimes arouse the soul of man.

Trapper

When Ben arrived at the scene of the massacre, the day after it had happened, it was a gruesome sight with blood all over the ground and barn. There had been some savage murders here last night. Mr. Jones was very distraught and almost in tears. The victims were the pride of his life and now they were gone, savagely killed, just because they were there. They were all bitten in the neck and their lifeblood drained from their bodies.

"Ben, what kind of devil could do this?" Mr. Jones asked, trying to put a meaning to such a massacre. Ben didn't answer right away. He was carefully looking for clues or sign of the killer.

"Mr. Jones, it ain't no devil, although it is as mean as a devil," Ben said.

"What is it Ben?" Mr. Jones pleaded. About that time, as Mr. Jones had his full attention on Ben, waiting for an answer, something flew down from the tree above, hitting Mr. Jones in the back. He let out an awful yell as he fell to the ground. The force of the blow wasn't enough to knock Mr. Jones down. It just scared him so bad that he fell.

Ben helped Mr. Jones up, who was now covered in blood, not from his attacker, but from the blood on the ground. Mr. Jones turned and saw the creature standing there, almost solid red, with great big spurs sticking out of its legs.

"Big Red!" Mr. Jones hollered and grabbed his big red rooster up and gave him a big hug. "I thought you were gone," he said, rubbing his prized rooster's head.

"Mink," Ben said. "He got in the pen looking for something to eat and found it."

"Why did he kill all my chickens? He didn't eat them?" asked Mr. Jones, still searching for some meaning to the bloody scene.

"Mink can get into a killing frenzy when they taste blood. He killed the first hen and would have eaten her if it had been the only one there. After he tasted the hot blood, he killed everything that moved. He would bite one on the neck and drop it as soon as he saw another one move. Then he would grab it and kill it and so on until every last one of your hens were dead."

"I had forty hens in this pen; one little mink couldn't have killed all of them," stated Mr. Jones.

"Oh yeah, a mink is a killing machine. He's quick as lightning, with sharp teeth made for puncturing flesh. His neck muscles are so strong that you could hit him with that hoe handle and it wouldn't even break his neck. But his brain isn't very big and his purpose is to kill and eat, but in a chicken pen where the hens can't run away, the only signal from his brain is kill–kill–kill," Ben informed Mr. Jones.

"I've got three more pens full of hens. If he kills all of them, I'll be out of business," Mr. Jones frantically stated.

"He killed last night. He'll be back to eat chicken breast tonight. If you want me to, I'll set a trap and catch him. Mink pelts are bringing twenty dollars right now. I'll be glad to catch him for you," said Ben.

"You catch him and I'll give you twenty more dollars just to see the little devil dead," said Mr. Jones.

"Deal," Ben said and shook Mr. Jones' hand.

Ben didn't waste any time getting started. He told Mr. Jones to put his rooster up, so he wouldn't get in the way and began surveying the situation.

"All these dead hens—which one are you going to eat Diablo?" he said to himself. After thirty minutes of studying the mass of dead chickens, "You're the lucky one for supper tonight," he said to the dead chicken or more to himself because the chicken really didn't care. This chicken was closest to the hole in the pen that the mink had come through. Ben knew that it was most likely that the mink would come back through the same hole and eat the first chicken it came across.

Ben carefully placed his trap in such a way that the mink would place both front feet in the trap when he came for supper. That way, there would be a sure catch and no need to worry about a trap–shy mink.

As Ben was on his way back from the pen, he saw Mr. Jones sitting on his porch.

"Mr. Jones, I'll be back to check my trap at daylight. You need to stay out from up there so you don't mess anything up," said Ben.

"How many traps did you set?" asked Mr. Jones anxiously.

"One," said Ben, holding up one finger.

"One? Don't you think you ought to set ten or twelve or twenty?" asked Mr. Jones, showing a definite lack of confidence.

"No, you don't need a dozen traps to catch one mink. If he comes back to eat tonight, he'll be in my trap in the morning," Ben said with assurance.

Ben showed up at Mr. Jones' right before daylight, knowing that Mr. Jones would be sitting on ready.

"Good morning, Ben," Mr. Jones called from the porch.

"Morning. You ain't been up at the pen already have you?" Ben teased Mr. Jones.

"No, I ain't been up there. You told me not to mess nothing up, but I sure am anxious to see that mink," said Mr. Jones.

"Well, let's go get him," said Ben with a smile.

They walked into the chicken pen and there he was. Just like Ben had planned, with both front feet in the trap.

"There he is Mr. Jones. Just like I said he would be," boasted Ben. Mr. Jones walked around the side looking at the little devil and the little devil was looking at him.

"He sure don't look like much, but I don't like those beady black eyes," said Mr. Jones.

He walked a little closer and Ben said, "Watch him. He might bite you on the neck and then you would be lying there like your chickens."

"Don't mess with me, boy. I want to get a good look at this thing." As Mr. Jones knelt down for a closer look, that mink jumped and growled at him and sent him stumbling back a few paces.

"That thing is mean," Mr. Jones said, keeping his distance from the mink. Ben was trying to keep from laughing out loud, but couldn't. Mr. Jones was really spooked.

Ben dispatched the mink, pulled his trap and left the massacred chickens for Mr. Jones to deal with later.

When they got back to the house, Mr. Jones said, "Wait just a minute and I'll get your twenty dollars from the house."

"You don't have to give me twenty dollars. I'll get twenty from this devil's hide." Mr. Jones ignored him and went on into the house.

When he came out he said, "A deal's a deal," and handed Ben a twenty dollar bill.

"I sure do appreciate that; you are a man of your word," said Ben.

"Thank you for catching that varmint and come back anytime you want," Mr. Jones said.

"I'll do that. I saw some fox sign back up on the side of that hill. I'll come lay some steel and see what I can catch. There's no telling what's up there trying to eat your chickens," Ben teased.

"Well, come lay your steel, Trapper. I need to keep the rest of my chickens alive," said Mr. Jones.

They said good bye and Ben drove down the road in his old Ford pickup. On the way home he was thinking, *Forty dollar day; we'll eat good this week*. Plus he had more land to trap on. Mr. Jones had given him right of way to all his land. That's how Ben obtained rights to a lot of land, by helping farmers with a problem animal and then the farmers helped him out by giving him rights to trap. It all worked out to the good and he kept his family fed and clothed, which was not an easy task; times were hard and jobs were few. Ben just did what he had to do. His Paw had told him once, "A man's got to do what a man's got to do," and Ben never forgot it.

The next morning, Ben was out an hour before daylight tending his trap lines. He was having a good day with two fox, one mink, a big boar coon, and several muskrats. It was a fine day to be a trapper. Fur prices were up and fur bearers were plentiful.

As he stopped off at the Bolton Swamp, he had high expectations. He had set beaver and otter traps there yesterday.

As he waded through the swamp, he heard something moaning. Stopping to listen, it was coming from behind the beaver dam. Wondering what it was, he eased over to the dam, thinking that it sounded like somebody, not something. It was somebody. Ben could see an arm sticking out from under some brush that had been thrown on top of whoever it was. Ben quickly removed the brush. It was Henry Wilks, a coon hunter that Ben knew.

Henry was cut up real bad and had lost a lot of blood. *I've got to do something quick,* Ben thought.

He took two long beaver sticks and tied some short sticks across them to make a stretcher. Then he eased Henry onto it and tied him down, so he wouldn't fall off on the way out of the swamp. Ben knew that he had to get going fast or Henry would die from loss of blood. He took one last look around and wondered, "What kind of animal could do this?"

Ben had thrown all his gear off, so he could move faster. There wasn't any good way to get Henry out; no way to drag him across the top of the beaver dams. So, he piled off into the cold water. All he could do was drag him through the water; some shallow and some so deep that he had to swim. All of it was cold and it didn't take long before Ben began getting numb. He was thinking, *Poor Henry's going to freeze to death if he doesn't bleed out first.*

It took thirty minutes for Ben to get Henry out of the swamp. Ben dragged him right up into the back of his pickup. Glancing at Henry's chalky white face, he knew that he had to hurry and jumped into his truck and took off. There was a doctor's office in town about eight miles to the north and a hospital about forty miles to the west. Ben didn't think that Henry could survive the forty mile trip, so he headed for Doc Harris' office.

Driving his truck right up to the front door, he went in hollering for help. Two men waiting in the office came out to help him.

"My goodness, that's Henry Wilks!" one of the men exclaimed.

"He's dead," the other man said.

"Good Lord, what happened to him?"

"I hope he ain't dead. I almost froze to death trying to get him here," said Ben.

Doc Harris met them in the hallway.

"Bring him back here," Doc said. "Lay him on his back on that table." Doc Harris went to work on him. "He's alive. He doesn't look like it, but he is. He's like a block of ice and soaking wet." Doc looked at Ben and noticed that Ben was wet and chilled.

"Was he in the river?" Doc asked.

"No," Ben said. "I found him in the Bolton Swamp." Ben hesitated and said, "Covered with brush." Doc looked up at Ben like someone had walked over his grave. Something from the past had come back to haunt him. Doc just stood there with a strange, blank look on his face. Finally, he snapped out of it and got to work on Henry.

"I've got to sew all these gashes up before he warms up or he'll bleed to death. It's a good thing that you kept him cool. You probably saved his life."

Doc worked on Henry six hours before he finished stitching him up. He came out of the room, looking for Ben with a very concerned look on his face.

"Ben, come back to my office. I need to ask you some questions." Ben followed Doc back to his office.

"Is he going to make it?"

"I think so, Ben. I did all I could do. He'll be moved to the hospital shortly. We don't need to be asking him any questions until he gets better," said Doc.

"Okay, but I've got some questions that need asking," said Ben.

Doc looked at Ben and said, "Don't go back into the Bolton Swamp."

"I've got traps and gear left in there. I've got to go back," said Ben.

"Just leave it. This isn't the first time this has happened, Ben! There's evil in that swamp and you'd best stay out," Doc warned Ben, fear clearly evident in his eyes.

"What are you talking about? If you know something about this, you better tell me because I ain't leaving my traps in there," Ben said.

Doc began, "Back when I was just a kid, about fifty years ago, I was sitting on my grandmaw's porch after supper one night. Grandpaw, Paw, and some of my uncles were out there smoking and telling stories. I always stayed to the back, out of the way, and listened. Those old stories always amazed me."

"One that has always stuck in my mind was the one about an old trapper found in the Bolton Swamp. Uncle Jay found him covered with brush. He told how he was cut all to pieces, dead, like a rabbit some animal had killed and covered until it could come back to eat it. No one ever figured out what happened or what did this to him. After a few years, I don't think anyone else ever believed it to be true, but it always stuck in my mind and I never went into the Bolton Swamp. I don't know what it was, but I imagined whatever it was, wasn't anything normal. Not a bear, not a big cat, something that you'd never imagine it to be. Now that this has happened, I know its true and that's why I'm telling you, don't go back in there!"

Ben's brain was really buzzing now. "Doc, this is all very strange and I wouldn't even believe a word you've said, but I did see Henry and I did drag him out of there and I am going back in there."

"I knew that's what you were going to say, but don't go back tonight. Wait till daylight tomorrow; I have a bad feeling in my bones."

"Okay," Ben said, not really wanting to go back in the dark anyway. "I'll wait until tomorrow. If I'm not out by dark, you come looking for me."

"If you're not out by dark, you're not coming out and I'll never go in after you," said Doc, dead serious.

The night was long, as long a night as Ben had ever had. Every possible solution and every imaginable reason had run through Ben's mind. There was no use trying to sleep; it just wasn't going to happen. Ben got up out of bed and made coffee. "Just be prepared," he thought to himself. "Be ready for anything and everything."

Ben was loaded for bear as he pulled up at the swamp in his old truck. He had his 30–30 rifle, 22 caliber single action six pistol, skinning knife, and a whole head full of wild thoughts. *Might as well get this over with,* he thought as he started into the swamp.

Easing along with eyes peeled, searching for any sign or movement, Ben silently closed the distance to where he had found Henry. No movement, sound, or sign of anything. No birds, squirrels, no wind, no nothing. Coming up to the pile of brush that had covered Henry, Ben noticed that something had been there and scattered the brush. Also the backpack that he had left was gone. The water at the edge of the beaver dam was still muddy. It had not been long since something had been there.

"Whatever was here got my pack and apparently was looking for Henry. So if I leave him—her—it— something else, it will come back, and if it is an animal, I can trap it," Ben rigged a noose right out in the open, but it was just a decoy. He then rigged another noose in the edge of the water to one side of the decoy. This one, designed to

catch it by the foot. The wire from the noose ran under water to a tree, then up the tree and over a limb. There it was fastened to a camouflaged barrel, which he had hung in the tree and filled with water. A trip wire ran from the barrel to the noose wire on the limb. When something moved the noose, it would trip the wire to the barrel full of water, down comes the barrel and up goes the noose with something's foot in it, simple as that. "Now, all I've got to do is persuade the foot," Ben said to himself.

Ben placed some of his gear on the beaver dam in such a way that something could come up to it in the water. Because, apparently whatever this thing was, it didn't like to leave the water. Placing a few limbs on each side to direct the foot into the noose, and the set was finished. Ben gathered his stuff up and left the swamp and swamp thing to the setting sun. *Tomorrow,* he thought *I'll have some answers.*

Another long night, that's two in a row, but Ben, did manage to sleep a few hours. Daylight came with even more anticipation than usual; today he was trapping the unknown.

The first rays of light found Ben in route to his swamp thing set. Halfway there, he stopped to listen. He could hear water splashing and brush thrashing. His veins were pumped full of adrenaline as he began to hurry his pace. .

Then there came a roar that shook the tree limbs around him. This stopped Ben dead in his tracks. Never had he heard anything like that. There was a loud pop and a splash, then silence.

Ben started running as fast as he could, but it was gone. There was water dripping off of everything and a steam filled the air. The limb was broken and the noose wire was wrapped around the tree. Something had put up a great struggle and had broken free from his trap. It wasn't very often that he set a trap that didn't work, but this one didn't hold. Ben was disappointed and yet somewhat relieved that he didn't have to deal with whatever had been in it.

Checking his noose to see what had failed brought an awesome discovery. There in the noose, was a toe or something like a toe. The creature that was in the noose must have been so heavy that it pulled its toe off. This was no ordinary toe; it was big, as big as Ben's hand. Real hairy and almost human looking, with a smell that was offensive, yet had a sweet musk to it.

Ben removed the toe from the noose and laid it down on a log at the edge of the water. Quickly, he gathered all his gear, and anxious to leave, turned to pick up the toe, but it was gone. He had just laid it there. He quickly looked all around him; no toe, no nothing, no sound, nothing seemed to be right. "I'm out of here," he said. "Nobody will believe this anyway."

As he turned to leave, he was struck across his chest by a tree limb. The force of the blow knocking the wind out of him, he landed on his back in the cold water. Opening his eyes in a half conscious daze, there was a tall hairy creature standing on the beaver dam, holding the tree limb.

Ben fought to stay conscious, after seeing what had happened to Henry, he new his fate would be sealed unless he did something quick. The creature started toward him as he reached for his pistol. The only chance he had was to put some lead into this thing before he could swing that limb again.

Ben freed the pistol from its holster just as the creature started down with the tree limb. He didn't have enough time to shoot before the limb would make contact with his head, so he quickly ducked his head underwater and raised his pistol at the same time.

He felt the limb strike him, but since he was underwater, the force of the blow wasn't as powerful. At the same time, he was firing his pistol blindly in the direction of the creature.

After empting his pistol, he surfaced for air, expecting another blow to the head, that didn't come. Almost to the point of unconsciousness, he managed to crawl out of the water and up on the beaver dam before darkness engulfed him.

Ben awoke to the pounding in his head, opened his eyes and realized where he was at. Raising the pistol, which he had miraculously managed to hold onto, he quickly surveyed his surroundings. The creature was nowhere to be seen and he wondered how long he had been unconscious.

Thinking more clearly now, he reloaded the pistol and noticed that there was blood in the water. Reaching up to feel of his head, revealed a large knot, but he wasn't bleeding. It wasn't his blood in the water; his shots must have found their mark.

An awful, musky scent filled the air and there was more blood on the beaver dam. He initially thought *I wounded it. I'll track him down and finish him,* but his whirling head was sending him a different message, a message that probably saved his life. He made his way back to the truck and headed for Doc Harris's office.

Four days later, after recovering from a concussion, Ben stopped by the hospital to see Henry Wilks. Upon entering the room, Henry, bandaged from head to toe, managed a smile, "Hello Ben. They told me what you did. Thank you."

Ben liked the coon hunter and felt compassion for him. "You would have done the same thing for me. How are you feeling?"

"Weak, but I'll recover," Henry said with assurance.

"Henry, I don't know if you saw what did this to you, but I saw it and I need to know, for my own sanity, that you saw the same thing."

"I didn't see it, Ben; it came from behind me. I had no idea that anything was even there until it grabbed me. It was tall. I know that it was tall because its hairy arms came down over my shoulders when it grabbed me. I could feel its huge body against me when it lifted me off the ground. After that, everything went black, until I woke up here in this room." Henry paused, "There is one thing that I will never forget though."

"What's that?"

"The smell." Upon hearing Henry's words, the scent of the creature instantly came back to Ben. It was a smell that would linger with him for the rest of his life.

"The smell was unforgettable and it was tall." Ben said. "It looked unlike anything that I have ever seen before, hairy like an animal, but stood upright and moved like a man. He hit me with a limb; an animal wouldn't know how to use a limb as a weapon. I don't know what it was."

Ben went on to explain in detail, the incident that had taken place in the swamp. Henry and Ben both vowed to return to Bolton Swamp to track the creature down and put an end to its aggressions, as soon as both of them fully recovered.

Ben and Henry, attempting to uphold their vow, returned to Bolton Swamp, searching high and low for some sign of the creature. There was no sign to be found, perhaps the reason this creature stays in or near the water. Water holds no tracks, just ripples, which quickly fade away and leave no evidence of the unknown....

> *The moral of this story is...*
> *The eyes of man sometimes see*
> *what the mind can not explain.*

Catfish

They call me Catfish, and rightly so I guess. I've caught every kind of catfish that ever swam up and down the Coosa River. Blue cats, Bull head blues, Yellow cats, Channel cats, Flatheads, Mud cats, Appaloosas and the most feared of them all, the Sharked Toothed Brahma Humping Bull cat.

They got their name from being so mean like a Brahma Bull, biting like a shark and if you ever got one of these fish into the boat, he would draw up in a hump and crap all over your boat. This is an awful mess and it stinks mighty fearsome. Then he'll lay there showing you his teeth and grinning. But don't try to pick him up; he'll snap your fingers off and hump up again, making another awful mess. Matter of fact, about the only thing they do is snap, hump, crap and grin. Now, let me tell you a little about myself and how I got the noble name of Catfish.

As far back as I can remember; I was two years old, born on the Coosa River in a river cabin. Paw gave the midwife a pig for lending a hand. Boy, I'm glad they didn't name me Porky. But my real name is Charles Hopping McGhee. In Indian my name is Charles Hopping on one Foot. Wilson, an old Indian friend of my Grandpaw, named me one day when he saw me hopping around the yard after I had stepped in dog mess—barefoot. I hate dog mess and I just can't understand why a dog has to mess in a place where I'm going to put my foot. Anyway, I never really liked either of those names, but when they nicknamed me Catfish, well, it just seemed to fit.

I was almost three when Paw and Grandpaw would catch a mess of catfish and bring em home. I would get right in there with them, pick them up and carry them around. Maw was a little worried at first that I would get one of those awful fins stuck in me. Paw told her, "Let the boy be. If he gets finned, it'll teach him a lesson." But I didn't and Paw started letting me fish with him.

Paw was a good fisherman and he taught me lots of ways to catch fish. So I took all of this and expanded on it. I developed new techniques and new baits. Why, I could probably write a book on everything I know about catching catfish, but I ain't. I'm not giving up my secrets to the whole world. I got to catching so many fish and so many big fish that I practically became famous. People from everywhere wanted to know how to do this and how to do that and I helped them out a little, but I didn't let 'em know everything. Once, *National Geographic* wanted me to go down to South America and Africa to catch some of those giant catfish, so they could get a picture and write a story. I went down there and caught the fish. It was so easy, like taking candy from a baby, and they paid me. But I had to lay low for a while after that. People wanted to do stories on me and wanted my autograph. Why, one man wanted me to sign his wife with permanent ink. Things got kind of crazy and were interfering with my fishing, so I laid low for a while.

The next stage of my life is kinda hard to write about because it was the happiest and saddest time of my life. But I guess the story would not be complete if I didn't tell of the love of my life. It was July, very hot and I was out on the river checking things out. You know, kinda like city boys do when they ride around the Dairy Queen. I just ride up and down the river.

Well, I was headed up river when I saw her. I think my heart stopped beating, my lungs stopped breathing and my jaws stopped working, because my mouth was wide open and I couldn't say a word. She was the most beautiful girl I had ever seen, her boat was broke down and she was waving at me to stop, but I was so stricken that I ran right by her. Finally, I got control of myself, spun that boat around on a dime and headed back to save my damsel in distress. She was standing there, in the boat, her hands on her hips with that look in her eye like, "I own you."

I pulled up alongside her boat with the skill of a sea captain and said, "H–h–h–h–h–hey."

She said, "What's wrong with you? Can't you talk?" and smiled like an angel. We instantly fell in love. If we were fishing, we were together; if we were swimming, we were together; if we were walking or talking or anything, we were together. Love had struck on the Coosa River and I was the victim. Cupid's arrow had pierced my heart and I was glowing like a shiny red tomato.

Those were two of the happiest years of my life. I woke every morning with a smile on my face and thought this is the way I'll spend the rest of my life. That's when it happened; that's when my heart was broken. The love of my life wouldn't be my wife. She said that she was tired of smelling fish all the time and knew that I would never stop fishing as long as I was alive. She was right about that and it wasn't long until she left with a Rock and Roll singer, who came through town one week. I moped around for a whole month, couldn't get going and couldn't eat right, generally just being useless.

I finally snapped out of it when an old friend, Red, came to see me. He cheered me up and we talked about old times and all the fish we had caught. I got to feeling better and told him, "Red, I learned a valuable lesson from all my sorrow."

"What's that Catfish? Never look at a woman again?"

"No," I said. "I'm not that busted up, but the next time I ask a woman out, the first thing I'm going to do is ask her if she likes fish. Then I'm going to spray some of that catfish cologne that I made awhile back, all over me and if she even acts like she don't like it, I'm carrying her home right then. I've done had one broken heart and don't intend on a replay."

Red called me back awhile later and said he needed my help. People down on the Wahelee River were having trouble with this Giant Catfish; he was eating all the ducks, dogs, bass and anything else that dared to swim in the waters. They had hired someone from up north, but he couldn't catch him. So I said that I would help him.

We got down there on the Wahelee River a week later, Red and me, and were setting our hook lines out. We had a fifty–five gallon drum for a float, five hundred pound test line and a hook used to catch Great White Sharks. Catching a twenty pound Peacock Bass to use for bait, we set the line a float in the river. I told Red, "We'll check it in the morning; he won't bite until midnight or later." About that time, the fifty–five gallon drum went under water. Red said he couldn't believe how aggressive this fish was and I agreed. We chased that fish for four hours and finally got hold of the line. Red was pulling up the line when all of the sudden, the giant fish jumped and landed right across the boat.

I couldn't believe what I saw. This was a mutant Shark Toothed Brahma Humping Bull Cat. He laid there grinning and I told Red, "Lookout Red; he's fixin to hump up!" But it was too late. That fish humped up and crapped all in the boat and just covered Red head to toe. Then he just slid back into the river, still grinning.

I had to work fast. That hump cat crap is some bad stuff. Red would be going into shock shortly if I didn't get him washed off and I knew I didn't want to give him mouth– to–mouth. So I grabbed Red and dragged him out of the boat, into the water and washed him clean. Finishing just before his lights were going out. Now we were faced with another problem. Swim or get back in the boat, half full of hump cat crap. We swam to shore, walked back to camp and loaded all our gear except the boat (which is still floating down the river somewhere) and headed back home.

Some people asked me if I felt like a failure, because I didn't catch that fish. I told them, "No, I didn't fail! You're talking to Catfish and Catfish don't fail when he's fishing."

"But you didn't catch that fish; he's still out there causing trouble to those people."

"He ain't still out there and Red and me are still alive. You see I had loaded the fifty–five gallon drum with dynamite and blew that hump cat into a million pieces. But not until he was a long way from us and we were out of the water and safely on shore."

"Oh, we understand now." I can't believe they doubted me, not Catfish McGhee.

This little adventure had me fired up again, so Red and I started a campaign to catch the world's meanest and largest catfish. We picked up a few sponsors, a couple of camera men and started our own T. V. show, *The Catfish and Red Show.*

The show was a big hit and we became even more famous. We caught the meanest, ugliest, biggest and most contrary catfish in the world. Why, we caught specimens that the scientist didn't even know existed.

We were rocking and rolling there for about ten years until we had caught every kind of catfish there was. Red, being a good business man had started up our own line of catfish bait and supplies. We made so much money that the luster kind of wore off and our hearts just weren't in the business anymore.

There were a couple of young fishermen who had watched every show that we had made and had turned out to be very good at catching catfish. We had met them on one of our film sites and became good friends, so we incorporated them into our show.

After nurturing them along until we thought that they were ready, we gave them the business. They have done quite well for themselves and I tune in to *The Catfish Academy* every week. It is a very interesting show and brings back fond memories of my youth, so I decided to head back home and wet my hooks in the Coosa River for the remainder of my life.

Well, things kinda tapered down after that and I mellowed out some. Fishing was still the biggest part of my life, but I only fished forty hours a week now and spent much of that time with young kids, teaching them how to catch fish. I started branching off socially by going to the movies, out to eat and even attended my high school reunion, which was fun.

I ran into Betty Bean, who I hadn't seen since we graduated high school. She was looking pretty good and we hit it off real quick. We started dating and had some good times there for a while, but it turned out that she didn't like fishing very much. Rather than going on with something that I knew wouldn't last very long, we parted ways. We get together every now and then just for laughs, but nothing serious ever came out of it.

But still, there was an empty spot in my heart for the love that I had lost. It's amazing how that can still bother me, but I suppose that I can understand. Love must be like the smell of that stinky catfish bait that I use, it just won't go away.

The moral of this story is ...
The smell of fish lingers with those
who have fish on their hands.

The Legend Of Lizzy

The date was 1965 and the place was the Coosa
River. Kit Sherman and his Paw, Don Sherman,
were out on the river in a homemade wooden
boat, armed with nothing but two paddles and
they were having a hard time of it.

It had been raining for a week and this was the
first chance they had gotten to run the trotlines.
The river was swollen out of its banks and none
of the lines could be found. Apparently, the logs
and stumps that had washed down the river had
torn all the lines out.

They were both getting quite a workout,
just trying to keep the boat going in the right
direction.

"Kit, grab that tree limb," Paw said as they
struggled with the boat, trying to paddle over to
the bank.

"I've got it." Kit grabbed the limb and tied a rope around it to hold the boat while they rested.

As they took a break from the strenuous paddling, Paw said, "We're going to have to rest up to be able to paddle back across the river. All the lines are gone anyway, we will have to put out new ones when the river goes back down."

They rested for awhile and were almost ready to paddle back across the river when Kit said, "Paw, look out there, there's some kind of animal washing down river." They could tell that it was struggling to stay alive. It kept going under and coming back up for air, but they couldn't tell what it was.

"Shove us off Kit," Paw said. He knew the animal couldn't last much longer by the way it was struggling. Kit untied the rope and off they went to rescue the poor critter.

As they approached it, Kit called out, "It's a dog and he's about had it!"

They paddled harder and came up along side of it. Kit grabbed a handful of hide on the dog's back and lifted it into the boat. The dog just lay there, trying to catch its breath. It was totally exhausted and near death.

Upon examining the dog, it appeared to be brown and white, but the muddy river water had stained the dog's hair and he couldn't be sure. Although the poor dog was soaked, muddy and almost dead, Kit noticed that it had an odd but proud look about it. Before he could finish his observation, Paw hollered "Paddle boy!" Kit picked up his paddle and helped Paw battle the raging river.

By the time they got to the other side of the river and pulled the boat up onto the bank, the small dog was trying to hold its head up.

"Paw, do you think it will live?" Kit asked.

"I don't know, maybe, it's pretty weak. There's no telling how long it's been in the water."

Paw picked up the soaked dog and examined it.

"It's a girl and a young one, probably half grown. She must have washed in around Big Bend where Cold Creek comes into the river. That's about four miles. If she survived that, I guess we ought to do everything we can to save her." Paw looked at the small dog and then out at the raging river and said, "That dog's got grit. Let's get her up to the house."

A week later, she was running around like nothing had ever happened. She appeared to have some feist and maybe some hound in her. About the size of a beagle, but with ears and snout similar to that of a feist dog, she was a very unique dog to say the least.

Kit had already formed a bond with the dog from the moment he lifted her out of the water.

"Dog, come here," he called to her and she came right away. "I've got to give you a name," he said as he petted the strange looking dog. "You kinda look like Paw's sister Lizzy. I'll call you Lizzy."

Paw heard Kit calling Lizzy and asked, "You think that your Aunt Lizzy looks like a dog?"

"No, sir, Paw," Kit answered quickly. "I just think the dog looks like Aunt Lizzy."

Paw laughed and said, "I think that you have a good dog there. If you want her to be loyal to you, you can do what your Grandpaw used to do with his dogs."

"What's that Paw?" Kit asked.

"Take a piece of bacon and put it in the sole of your shoe early in the morning. She'll smell it and follow you around all day. At the end of the day, take it out and feed it to her. She will be loyal to you to the day she dies." Kit did just as Paw told him to do and it worked. Wherever you saw Kit, you saw Lizzy. It seemed to be her purpose to be at his side.

One day Kit was feeding the cattle, which was his daily chore. The Shermans ran around fifteen head of blackish brown cattle, which consisted of cows, steers and one herd bull. The bull was solid black and had been quite temperamental since he had run off, getting into someone's whisky still and becoming intoxicated. You never knew what to expect out of that bull and Paw had warned Kit to be cautious. He had busted a bale of hay open and was scattering it out for the cows when he noticed that their herd bull was acting strange. Then he got worried because the bull started pawing the ground and shaking his head from side to side.

Kit started to back out of the pen, but, it was too late; the bull charged him and he was too far from the gate to get out of the pen. He tried to dodge the bull, but the bull slung his head sideways, knocking Kit down in the dirt and turned quickly to mash Kit down in the ground with his massive head.

Kit looked up to see the bull's crazed eyes as he was almost upon him. His life was flashing before his eyes and he thought, *This is it!* The bull rolled him one time, but then whirled away from him. Lizzy was locked onto the bull's tendon just above his back hoof. The bull was frantically kicking and bucking, trying to shake the dog from his leg, which gave Kit time to get up and out of the pen.

Lizzy was being violently thrashed around, but would not release her hold on the bull's leg. Paw heard the commotion and came out of the house with his shotgun. He fired two loads of birdshot into the bull, which stopped his frantic flight.

Kit called Lizzy and finally got her to release her hold on the bull. She was so badly shaken up that she couldn't walk, but crawled out of the pen, while keeping an eye on the bull.

"Are you okay?" Paw asked Kit.

"Yes, sir, but Lizzy's not." Every joint in that dog had been dislocated.

Paw looked at that bull and said, "You're going to the butcher." Then he looked down at Lizzy and said, "That dog's got grit."

Kit gently picked Lizzy up. He could see the pain in her eyes, yet she didn't even whimper. As far as he could tell, no bones were broken, which was a miracle, after the thrashing that she had taken. Although she was stretched, had dislocated joints, was bruised internally and in much pain, she still had that proud look about her. Kit rubbed her head saying "Good girl." showing his approval to his loyal dog, which was all that she really wanted.

Kit made her a comfortable bed and did everything that he could possibly do to help her. He had to pick her up and carry her out in the yard to do her business because she couldn't walk. She wasn't hungry, but would eat just because she knew that Kit wanted her to and slowly began to regain her strength.

A week after the calamity, Paw, busily taking care of business around the farm, saw Lizzy out in the yard. Upon seeing her, he stopped what he was doing, watching her painfully crawl across the yard to do her business in the same place that Kit had been carrying her to.

Finished, she turned and crawled back to her bed. As Paw watched, he could see her wincing in pain with every movement, yet she continued her arduous journey. With great respect, he smiled and shook his head, thinking, *that dog's got grit.*

Lizzy slowly began walking and wagging her tale again as her elated master worked with her every day. Eventually making a full recovery, strengthening the bond between her and Kit. A bond so strong that only death could sever. Word got around about Lizzy saving Kit from the bull and when Fred Simmons heard about it, he had to see that dog. Fred was a coon hunter and had owned some of the best dogs in the state, but had never heard of a dog doing something like that.

Fred came by the Sherman's the very next day. "Hello, Don. How are you doing?"

"Howdy, Fred. I figured you'd be coming by."

"Why's that?" Fred asked, like he didn't know. Paw called for Kit to come and bring Lizzy, which was automatic because Lizzy was always with Kit.

Fred looked at Lizzy and said, "What in the world kind of dog is that?"

"She's the best dog in the world," Kit proudly proclaimed. "But what breed is she? I don't know."

"That's the strangest looking dog that I've ever seen. Will she tree coons?"

"I don't know," Kit said. "But I bet she will. She'll do anything I tell her to."

"Well, why don't you bring her and come coon hunting with me tonight? If she will attack a bull like that, she might make one heck of a coon dog."

That night Fred came by and picked up Kit and Lizzy in his old truck. Fred had two of his best dogs in the dog box in back of the truck. He got out to open the box to put Lizzy in, but Kit let him know that Lizzy didn't ride in no dog box and got in the front of the truck with Lizzy in his lap.

Fred looked bewildered, but went along with it because he had to see what this dog would do. He drove down to Beaver Creek and told Kit, "I'll turn Blue and Hank out first, to show Lizzy what she's supposed to do. Here's a leash to put her on to hold her till Blue and Hank tree a coon."

"She don't need a leash. She'll stay right beside me until I tell her different," Kit said.

Fred looked bewildered again, but said, "Okay, let's go."

Fred turned his dogs out and they made four loops around the truck, scented everything up and then closed in on Lizzy. Lizzy stood her ground although she was half the size of the big hounds and let out a low growl. Fred laughed, "She won't take no crap," and called his dogs to the trail.

It didn't take long for Blue and Hank to strike a coon. They were on one hot and heavy. The bark of those hounds echoing through the night was a beautiful sound and Kit could tell that Fred was proud of his dogs, as he watched him listening in the dim light of his carbide lamp.

The dogs went almost out of hearing and Fred said, "They're on a boar coon. Let's get in the truck and head them off." They jumped in the truck and drove about a mile down the road and stopped to listen. "Listen. They're treed. Let's go get them."

Blue and Hank were really hammering down on that tree when they got there. Both of the dogs were gnawing on the tree like they could chew it down. Fred turned his carbide lamp up and spotted the coon up in the fork of the tree.

"Woo–wee! Look at the size of that boar. I'll squall him down and we'll see one heck of a fight."

Fred squalled to the coon and he knew what he was doing, because that coon started coming down that tree. He stopped about ten feet from the ground and started growling at the hounds. Then all of the sudden, he jumped off on them, landing right on top of Blue's head. That coon sunk his teeth in Blue's nose and Blue let out the most awful sound that Kit had ever heard.

The fight was on and the coon was getting the best of it. Hank jumped in, but missed the coon and latched onto Blue's ear by mistake. The coon seized the opportunity, released its grip on Blue's nose, jumped on Hank's head and commenced to shred Hank's ear which brought on another awful yelp.

Blue jumped back just glad to be free from the coon's grip, while Hank was trying to shake the coon off of his head. Finally, the coon let go and ran off. Maybe he thought that he had inflicted enough pain on the two dogs. While Blue and Hank were hesitant about chasing him, Fred urged them on and the chase was on again.

Fred looked at Kit and said, "That was the baddest coon I've seen in a long time. I guess old Lizzy doesn't have it in her. She didn't want any part of that coon."

Kit replied, "I didn't tell her to get it. I figured old Blue and Hank could handle the situation. Did you want her to help them?"

Fred looked at Kit, who was standing there grinning and said, "Come on, let's go."

With that, they took off on the trail of the two barking hounds. The coon didn't go very far this time. He had run about as far as he was going to. If those dogs wanted some more of him, here he was. When they got to the tree, the coon was standing on a low limb, all bristled up and growling at the dogs.

Fred looked at Kit and said, "All right, this time I'll squall him out and you tell Lizzy to get him."

"Okay," said Kit. "But you don't have to squall him out. I'll send Lizzy up to get him. He's no more than ten feet off the ground. Lizzy can climb that high."

"All right then!" Fred's feelings may have been hurt a little bit. "Do it!" Well, Kit told Lizzy to get the coon and Lizzy started circling the tree, looking up at the coon, surveying the situation.

Fred laughed, "What's she going to do; circle the tree for seven days and then it will fall down like the walls of Jericho?"

Kit looked at Fred and said, "Maybe you had better put your dogs on those leashes, so they don't get hurt when the tree falls."

Fred had his dogs leashed and Lizzy was still circling the tree.

"Okay, Lizzy, get him girl!" Lizzy ran back behind Kit and got a running start. She hit that tree so fast that she just ran right up it, all the way to the coon, snatching the coon off of the limb. Lizzy and the coon hit the ground in a big ball of rolling, squalls, yelps, growls, teeth gnashing, fur flying and blood slinging fury. Fred just stood there in amazement. He couldn't believe what he was seeing.

The fight went on for awhile and ended up in the creek. There was some splashing at first and then there was silence.

Fred hollered, "You better get that dog out of there or that coon will drown it." Fred and Kit ran up to the creek bank and shined the light down in the water. All that could be seen was

Lizzy's tail and the only movement was an occasional jerk.

Kit climbed down the creek bank and waded out to his dog, grabbing her by the tail to drag her out. He pulled Lizzy, with the coon still attached to her, up on a sand bar. Lizzy had the coon by the neck and the coon had Lizzy's front leg in his mouth.

Fred ran down to the sandbar and stammered, "That's the beatingest thing I ever saw! Look at them, neither one will let go!" Lizzy had the better end of the deal and was slowly choking the life out of the coon.

"A coon like that deserves to live. He can breed some more bad coons to keep your dogs on their toes." Kit looked at Fred and Fred nodded in agreement.

Kit put his hand on Lizzy's back and said, "Okay, girl, let him go." Lizzy cut her eyes back toward Kit and started loosening her grip on the coon's neck. You could hear the coon taking a deep breath as its windpipe opened and his jaws relaxed from around Lizzy's leg. The coon slowly got to its feet and looked at Lizzy, but didn't growl because he didn't want anymore of that dog. He turned and slowly headed down the creek with

Lizzy watching him and Lizzy was hoping that coon didn't turn around and come back either.

Back at the truck with all the dogs loaded up, Fred said, "If I had not seen that with my own two eyes, I'd never believe it. That dog's got grit! I'll give you fifty dollars for her right now."

"She's not for sale, Fred, and she never will be. Now take us home. Lizzy and me did all the work tonight and we're tired."

Word got around about Lizzy's ability as a coon dog and every coon hunter for miles around wanted Kit and Lizzy to go hunting with them. Some of them were offering five hundred dollars for her, but Kit didn't care if it was five thousand, he wasn't going to sell her. He finally gave in to breed her with one of Fred's small hounds and she had five fine looking puppies. Giving Fred the pick of the litter, he kept the rest for himself.

Kit slacked off on coon hunting to give Lizzy time to raise her pups. They played and slept and played some more. Eventually, Lizzy started taking them off on training sessions down by the river. They would bay frogs and turtles and run all the birds and ducks off like any young dogs coming of age. Everything was going along just fine, until they had an incident down on the river banks.

Lizzy came back to the house with just three puppies, made them stay and ran back down to the river. Kit saw that she had lost a puppy and took off down there. Lizzy kept on running up and down the shore looking and sniffing, but there was no puppy to be found. They kept looking until dark without any luck and then returned to the house.

Kit told Paw what had happened and Paw thought that the puppy had gotten in the river and drowned. He said that they would go down in the morning and take a look. Kit wanted to go back down that night, but Paw told him that if the puppy didn't drown, they would find him in the morning. That was a long night for Kit and an even longer night for Lizzy.

Early the next morning, Paw and Kit went down to the river to look. Lizzy was already there, running up and down the bank in the same place she had been the day before. There was no sign of the puppy, but there were some strange looking tracks on the bank. Kit didn't know what they were and Paw thought that they looked like beaver tracks, but not exactly.

"I don't think a beaver would have got the dog, but something has been going on here," said Paw.

They finally gave up the search and started back to the house when they heard Lizzy start raising cane.

Kit said, "Something is down there; I know that bark!" They ran back down to the river in time to see Lizzy charging into the water. Kit saw what it was then: a big gator. He tried to call Lizzy off, but she thought that the gator had her puppy and would stop at nothing to get it back.

She jumped right on top of his head and the gator's jaws snapped shut on Lizzy's front leg. Paw and Kit watched helplessly as the gator dragged Lizzy out into the water, but they could see that Lizzy had sunk her teeth into one of the gator's eyes. There was an awful thrashing and rolling as they went under in the deeper water. Kit's heart sunk as the bubbles floated to the surface. He had lost his beloved dog, the faithful dog that saved his life years ago.

They were standing there in silence when Lizzy's head popped up. "She's alive!" Kit shouted, as Lizzy was swimming back to the bank. Paw jumped into the water and waded out to get her because she wasn't swimming very well. The gator had bitten her leg off just above the knee, but she had the gator's eye in her mouth. The gator came up shaking his head back and forth as he swam away.

They carried Lizzy back to the house and laid her on the kitchen table. "We've got to do something. She's bleeding bad!" Kit pleaded. Paw covered her with a blanket and stuck his big hunting knife on the stove.

"We've got to cauterize that leg or she will bleed to death," said Paw. As soon as the knife got red hot, Kit held Lizzy down and Paw stuck the hot knife to Lizzy's leg. She yelped and lost consciousness as the terrible stench of burning flesh filled the air. Paw stood back when he had finished, looking at Lizzy and said, "That dog's got more grit than anything I ever saw."

Lizzy survived the ordeal with the gator, which Paw later killed and tanned its hide. They now knew what had happened to the lost puppy and Kit thought that it would be too much on Lizzy, raising the other puppies with just three legs, so he gave them away. Of course there were plenty of coon hunters that wanted them, so that wasn't a problem, but Kit wondered if Lizzy would ever be the same.

Lizzy struggled at first, but there was no giving up in that dog. Before long, she was getting around on three legs almost as good as she had on four. Kit even started carrying her hunting again and the coons sure were sorry for that. She still had her grit; it was just a little bit slower now.

Later that year, Fred wanted Kit to go canoeing down the Pea River, down in south Alabama. Kit told him that he didn't think he could make the trip, until Fred said, "You can bring old Lizzy with you. It will take about a week to go down it and I'll need some good company if I have to hang around with you all week."

"Well now, that's different; it will take both Lizzy and me to keep you out of trouble for a whole week," Kit countered.

Fred and Kit rounded up all their gear and supplies, loaded up the truck and lit a shuck. Which is a term used for getting an early start. The old–timers would sometimes start before daylight, setting a shuck of corn on fire to enable them to see.

First they went down to the take out point and found somebody that would go with them back up river and drive the truck back down. Ben Tiller was his name. He was about seventy years old and full of stories about growing up along the banks of the Pea River. It was a pleasure for Kit and Fred, making the one hour ride back up the river with Ben and he gave them a lot of tips about where to watch for danger and good places to camp.

Lizzy took to liking Ben on the ride up and Ben liked her back, scratching the top of her head and talking to her. Lizzy was eating that up.

"That's a mighty fine dog you have there. How did she lose her leg?" he asked. Kit filled him in on the story of Lizzy and the gator. Then he backed up and told Ben about finding her in the Coosa River, the bull, and coon hunting.

"Well, I'll be danged!" Ben said. "I've heard about that dog. She's a legend among the hunters and outdoorsmen down here. I really didn't know whether to believe the stories or not. Did she really gnaw that gator's eye out?"

"She sure did—pulled it right out of his head!" Fred proclaimed proudly as though Lizzy was his dog.

"That's one gritty dog. Ya'll had better watch out for hogs around that river. There are some big boars around and I've seen what those tusks can do to a dog. I'd hate to see old Lizzy have her days ended by a hog after all she's been through."

"She can hold her own," Kit said. "But thanks for the warning."

Arriving at the put in site, they put the canoe in the water, loaded all the gear, and said good-bye to Ben. He would be waiting to pick them up down river in seven days. As they started paddling down stream, Lizzy walked back and forth until she found her spot on the front of the canoe. She was sitting up there on the very front deck of the canoe like an emblem on a car hood, taking in all the scenery.

It was a pleasant trip, seeing all the wildlife and beauty of nature. They came around a bend in the river and there was a coon standing on a log that lay out in the river. Lizzy's hair bristled up and she turned to look at Kit.

Kit shook his head, "Not today old girl. We're observing, not hunting." Lizzy kept her eye on the coon until it ran out of sight into the bushes. She really wanted to chase it, but she was obedient to her master.

The trip went smoothly, with lots of sights to see and they found some good campsites. On the fourth day, as they got underway that morning, Lizzy's ears perked up and then they heard it. Snorting, huffing and thrashing around and then someone hollered "Help!" Fred and Kit paddled faster to get down to where the ruckus was going on and then they saw what was happening.

A young boy in his teens was barely holding on to a small tree, just out of reach of a big boar hog with tusks that stuck out of the sides of his mouth like two knifes. The hog was slashing at the boy and about to push the tree down. They had to act quickly.

"Get him!" Kit hollered and Lizzy bailed out of the front of the canoe into the water.

In a flash, she was on the bank and closing in on the hog. Kit was right behind her and Fred was getting the gun. Lizzy hit the hog wide open and just bounced off. The hog turned on her and came dangerously close with those huge tusks. She had given the young boy a diversion and he dropped out of the tree and took off running, but the hog turned on him and was closing in.

Lizzy made a three–legged dash (that was as fast as any four–legged greyhound) and locked onto the hog's tail. That hog turned round and round, like a helicopter, trying to sling the dog off, but Lizzy wasn't letting go. Finally, I guess that the hog had gotten dizzy and stopped to catch his breath, with Lizzy still attached to his tail. That was all the time that Fred needed and he quickly dispatched the hog with his rifle. It was over.

The young lad, whose name was Jimmy, was all right, though scared half to death, turned out to be Ben Tiller's grandson. He had been fishing on the river bank when the hog attacked him. Kit and Lizzy walked him back to his home, which was about a mile away, because he was too shaken up to do it alone.

Upon returning to the river, Fred had removed one of the loins from the hog's back and was grinning.

"I guess we'll have pork chops tonight." Kit laughed and Lizzy barked; another close call.

The rest of the trip went smooth as silk. Ben Tiller was waiting on them at the landing, but he wasn't alone. Jimmy was there, along with twenty other people to greet them. There was a great commotion as they pulled up to the landing. Everyone was trying to pet Lizzy and shake Fred and Kit's hands. Ben Tiller handed Kit a small sack with something in it and said, "Here's you a little souvenir from your trip." Kit opened the sack and there were the tusks that had been taken out of the boar hog's mouth. .

He looked at Ben and said, "Thanks!" Ben was smiling.

Kit and Fred didn't even have to load the truck. Everyone there pitched in to help and then followed them downtown. They didn't even have to drive. Ben drove and everyone else followed. It was like a parade coming into town. Ben pulled the truck up to the town's only café and people started coming out to see the legend that they had heard about.

They ate a fine meal, courtesy of the café owner. Pictures were taken, Lizzy got petted so much that Kit thought her hair might start falling out, and the local reporter was doing a story: "Jimmy Tiller Saved from the Jaws of Death by Three–Legged Dog!" This was a good ending to a great adventure on the Pea River.

Kit returned home and told the whole story in detail to Paw, who was petting Lizzy the whole time. *The legend of Lizzy is growing,* he thought to himself, *That dog's got grit.*

Life on the Coosa returned to normal: fishing, hunting, swimming, and farming. Ah, those were the good old days. Lizzy was fourteen years old, Kit had married and had two fine sons, Eric and Tad. He built a house and lived on the edge of Paw's land, teaching his sons the art of surviving on the river. Lizzy didn't hunt much anymore. Her joints were stove up from various beatings she had taken during her life and what a life it was, full of spine tingling adventures, every moment of it. The legend of Lizzy had grown statewide and often there were people coming by just to get a look at her.

Coyotes had started to become a problem along the Coosa River. I guess they had migrated in from the west and were wreaking havoc among the farmer's crops and livestock. Fred had been trapping them some, but they were overrun with them. One night a whole a pack of them hit Paw's chicken pen. Upon hearing the commotion, Lizzy took off over there, not as fast as she once was, but still trying.

The coyotes had already killed most of the chickens when Lizzy plowed into them. There were seven or eight coyotes, but that didn't deter Lizzy in the least. She grabbed the first one she came to and started shaking it. Seeing what had happened, the other coyotes jumped on her, ripping flesh, and cracking bones. By the time Paw got out there with his gun, it was too late for Lizzy. She had made her last stand, (fighting to her death.)

Paw started shooting and got a couple of the coyotes before they ran off, but one of them didn't run. Lizzy had it by the neck and died with the coyote still in her mouth. Paw looked down at Lizzy like he had many times before, but this would be the last time. He could barely get the words out through the sadness that he felt.

"That dog's got grit," he murmured.

About a month later, Fred came by to see Kit. They sat and talked about the good old days and the adventures that they had had.

Before Fred left he told Kit, "I've got something for you out in the truck." They walked out to the truck with the boys tagging along.

Fred walked around the truck to the dog box and pulled out a young dog. Kit was having a flashback. This dog looked just like Lizzy and the boys ran to her and started petting her.

"Remember Lizzy's puppy that you gave me years ago?" Fred asked. "Well, this is her puppy." Fred smiled.

"The legend lives on." Kit was grinning from ear to ear as he thought to himself, *here we go again!*

The moral of this story is…
Faithful companions of men sometimes bark.

Fishing With Fred

Fred was a very good friend of mine who loved life and his greatest passion was fishing. A generous man, who loved to share his philosophies of life while catching fish.

Fred considered himself a 'self poet' and would sometimes recite verse while doing something that he loved to do, which was, you guessed it, fishing. Therefore, the only pertinent way to describe Fred's life is with a poem.

Fishing with Fred,
Ah, what a treat.
He always catches something,
We were sure to eat.

A fly on his rod,
Or a tug on his string,
Happiness to Fred was…
Something a fish could bring.

No matter the weather,
No matter his wife.
Fred fished all the time,
That was his life.

One day it was bass,
The next it was bream.
Whatever he fished for,
He filled to the rim.

The day the boat had sunk,
Was just another day.
He dipped it out with a can,
And went fishing in the bay.

When Fred was just a lad,
He fished everyday there was,
And when he had grown older,
He'd go fishing just because.

I went with Fred one day,
To go fishing in the creek.
We caught fish all day long,
And decided to stay a week.

When the preacher man was hungry,
Or the clerk down at the store.
Fred would catch a mess of fish,
And be knocking on their door.

One day there had been,
A calamity at the lake.
Some guy came from town,
And Fred's boat, he did take.

Fred said bring my boat,
And tie it to this stump,
Or I will take my paddle,
And on your head, make a lump.

The fellow returned the boat,
And everything worked out.
Fred decided to go fishing,
And paddled all about.

Fred called on me one morning,
To help him catch some bait.
And when we got that finished,
We made a fishing date.

To go down to the river,
And bait up all the hooks.
Then catch some giant catfish,
And stack them up like books.

The skies were kind of cloudy,
And lightning struck afar,
Thunder boomed so loudly,
As Fred reeled in a gar.

As the storm grew closer,
I reeled in my line.
I was a little concerned,
But Fred was feeling fine.

Lightning struck a tree,
Then a rock on the bank.
Fred just kept on fishing,
Until his rod, gave a yank.

He had hooked a big one,
It almost pulled him in,
And when he almost had him,
Lightning struck him on the chin.

Fred's days had just been numbered,
Now we lay him down to rest.
In his fishing clothes, we dressed him,
That's how he looked his best.

Fred will always be remembered.
I put an old lure in his hand.
Then we closed the casket lid,
And laid him in the sand.

In summary of this poem, I would like to add that Fred was a great man and a great fisherman. He could catch fish under the most adverse conditions. I would venture to say that he could get a bite out of a mud puddle; he was that good.

Catching fish gave him great pleasure and he shared this with many people whose lives he touched. Fred the fisherman, poet and philosopher, left his mark on this world and did so with much passion, all the way to the end.

The moral of this story is …
Fishing, the experience,
is more than just wetting a hook.

Goat Island

Uncle Abe sat on the steps of his porch, carving a fishing lure out of a piece of wood with his pocket knife. He would be going fishing tomorrow and needed an extra lure.

It was Friday evening and my best girl Diane and I drove by and saw Uncle Abe sitting on his porch whittling. I slowed my old truck down and carefully pulled up in his yard, not wanting to cover Uncle Abe with dust.

I jumped out and told Diane to stay in the truck, that I would be right back. She said, "Okay," with no argument.

"Hey, Uncle Abe. What's happening?"

Uncle Abe looked around behind him and then back at me. "What does it look like is happening? Nothing."

"Well, it looks to me like you lost your old lure. Probably a big old bass hit it and was too much for you to handle. She broke you off again, didn't she?" I prodded at him.

"I'm going to catch that bass if it's the last thing I do!" he said as he began to whittle faster.

"Uncle Abe, I've been thinking about your situation. That's four times that she has broken your line, right?"

"Eight times!" he exclaimed as he stopped whittling and looked up at me. "She has done took eight of my lures." He was getting a little excited now. "Do you know how much whittling it takes to make eight lures?"

"Not as much as it takes to make nine," I laughed. He didn't think that was too funny from the look that he gave me, which was the reaction that I had hoped for. We liked to go on at each other—it made things more interesting.

"I think I'll go out to the point of Goat Island and see if I can catch her in the morning," I said, knowing that would stir him up a little more and it did.

"You stay away from there! I've got a score to settle with that bass and I better not catch you out there. You're not too big to tote a good whupping!" He let me know and I didn't doubt him.

The screen door opened and Aunt Lilly came out, all bent over sweeping the floor.

"If this broom gets any shorter, I'll have to get down on my knees to sweep. Abe, I think my broom handle is shrinking," She complained.

"You're just getting taller," said Uncle Abe as he looked up at me with a twinkle in his eyes.

"Lands sake," said Aunt Lilly as she straightened up and saw me. "Randy, I didn't know you were out here. Is that Diane out there in your truck?"

"Yes, ma'am."

"Tell her to get out and ya'll come set a spell."

"We can't stay. We're going across the creek to the dance tonight," I told her, and she walked over to the truck to talk to Diane.

Uncle Abe was still diligently working on his lure.

"Uncle Abe, what kind of wood is that?" He stopped his whittling, grinned at me and went right back to creating his work of art.

Uncle Abe, over the period of six years, had been secretly sawing a piece of Aunt Lilly's broom handle off to make his lures out of. After he sawed it off, he would take his pocket knife and round it back off, then take dirt and rub on it making it look like as though nothing had happened. I wondered how long he could keep doing this before Aunt Lilly caught on, and what she would do to him when she did.

"I've got it figured out Uncle Abe."

"What?" he questioned me.

"I know how you can catch that bass." This got his attention and he stopped whittling and looked up at me. "We can camp out on Goat Island next week. That way you can fish for that bass every morning at daylight and every evening right at dark. I'll paddle while you fish. You're sure to catch her if we do that."

I could see that he was thinking real hard about it. "What will we do the rest of the time?" he asked.

"Well, besides fishing, I guess we'll just..." I paused for a moment, thinking about what else we would do and then it came to me: "Fish!"

He raised his eyebrows and said, "Sounds good to me."

"Do you need to ask Aunt Lilly if you can go?" I poked at him.

"You better get out of here, boy, before you start some trouble. I'll meet you Monday morning down at the boat."

I woke up Monday morning to someone beating on my window. Raising up to look out the window, I saw Uncle Abe. I raised the window and asked him, "What time is it?"

"It's three o'clock. Get up, we got to go." Uncle Abe was in a hurry this morning and I found out why a week later.

He had left Aunt Lilly a note on the kitchen table: "Gone camping on Goat Island. Be back in a week. Love, Abe," and he wanted to be in the boat and gone before Aunt Lilly had a chance to read that note.

Uncle Abe had already loaded the gear in the boat when I walked up.

"Get in and let's go," he demanded.

"Did you get everything?" I asked.

"Yes, I got everything we need. Now let's go," he said as he hopped in the boat and told me to shove off.

"It sure is dark out here. I can't even see where we're going," I commented.

"I can find my way to Goat Island with my eyes closed. You just paddle and I'll navigate." He was right; pulled us up on the island exactly where he wanted to be, just before day break.

It was getting light as we unloaded our gear and set up camp.

"Did you bring water?" I questioned him, not seeing any.

"Dangit! I forgot the water."

"That's all right," I said. "I'll paddle you around the point while you fish and then we'll go back to your house and get some water."

"No! We can't do that. I mean—it's too far to paddle. We'll drink river water." I had an idea that Uncle Abe didn't want to see Aunt Lilly this morning.

With camp set up, we got in the boat and I paddled Uncle Abe around the point where that big bass lived. He cast his lure with great expertise, beside a log that lay out from the point, gently twitching it, to make it look like an injured minnow.

After twitching it four or five times, the water exploded as the bass sucked his lure in. Uncle Abe set the hook and the fight was on.

"Hold her!" I said as I paddled backwards to get the fish away from the log.

"I've got her this time!" Uncle Abe exclaimed, as he pulled the fish into open water. Then the fish made a run like a torpedo being shot out of a submarine. The line tightened as he tried to hold on and it sounded like a twenty–two rifle when it snapped.

Uncle Abe sat there with a defeated look on his face and I knew better than to take this opportunity to rag him on.

All was silent until Aunt Lilly's voice echoed across the water, "Abe, Abe Horton! Where are you?" Her calls faded away and Uncle Abe hadn't even heard them for he sat there staring at that log or maybe just staring. He had suffered a crushing defeat at the hands (or should I say tail) of a fish and had lost his last broom handle lure.

The silence was broken as the huge bass leapt from the water, shaking its massive head, trying to dislodge the lure from her lip. As she shook her head, the lure came loose and landed smack in the middle of Uncle Abe's lap.

This perked him up. At least he had his lure back and I couldn't help but laugh. She had soundly whupped him and then threw his lure back at him as if sending him a message or an insult. I don't know which, it being hard to read the mind of a fish.

Uncle Abe regained his composure and said, "That fish weighs twelve pounds."

"That was a big bass, but twelve pounds? I don't know if she weighs that much."

"Sure she does," he said with certainty.

"How do you know?" I quipped back at him.

"Well, she had scales on her side didn't she?" He had a point there, the fish did have scales and you do use scales to weight fish, but I don't know how he read them; I couldn't.

"I heard Aunt Lilly calling you awhile ago. Do you want to go back and see what she wanted?" I asked.

Uncle Abe said, "I didn't hear nothing," and started paddling back to camp.

Arriving at camp, we took care of the most important things first, setting out some catfish poles being the first order of business. We caught some night crawlers, baited our hooks and sat down on an old log to relax. There were fish jumping, an eagle sailing around in circles up in the sky, waiting for one of the fish to slip up and squirrels scurrying around in the trees. This was the life.

"Looks like we're not the only ones fishing," I commented as we watched the eagle. Uncle Abe just grunted his acknowledgement. Sometimes you just about had to pry words out of his mouth.

"Uncle Abe, have you ever seen one of those eagles actually catch a fish? I don't believe that I've ever seen an eagle catch a fish."

"Yep. They just don't want anyone to see them and move in on their fishing hole."

"I don't believe that. If that eagle could catch a fish right now, he would do it. He wouldn't pay any attention to us."

"You better believe it."

"Why?"

"Because you ain't never seen one catch a fish and that eagle ain't starving to death, is he? You talk too much. Now hush up and let me enjoy the peace and quiet."

We sat there and relaxed and listened. I guess Uncle Abe had a point. You can't hear a lot of the stuff going on around you if you're talking all the time.

After catching a mess of catfish and cleaning them, we set into the task of preparing supper, which was a three course delight: fried catfish, pork & beans and loaf bread. Nothing like a good meal to complement a day on the river.

I gathered a bunch of sage grass and small branches to make a comfortable bed under the tarp that we had tied between some trees. Uncle Abe was busy constructing a makeshift hammock out of another piece of tarp and some rope.

"Uncle Abe, that thing don't look too safe to me. I'll make you a bed under the tarp if you want me to." He didn't even look up, but kept working on his hammock.

"I ain't sleeping on the ground. Everybody knows that red bugs can't climb and I don't want no snake curling up with me tonight. You just sleep on your bed and I'll sleep in mine," he said rather rudely.

Uncle Abe didn't like anyone telling him what to do or even suggesting a better way. Aunt Lilly was the only one who could do that and I think that he was enjoying being "King of the Island."

I laid down on my makeshift bed, which I must say was an engineering feat and heard Uncle Abe fumbling around, trying to get into his state of the art hammock.

"Goodnight Uncle Abe," I said. He just grunted and continued fumbling around in the dark. I fell asleep listening to Uncle Abe still trying to get comfortable.

I was awakened at about 1:00 a.m. by a thud on the ground, then a commotion in the bushes, ending with a big splash in the river.

Jumping up, I grabbed the flashlight and heard Uncle Abe calling, "Help! Help!" I ran down to the river bank to find him trying to keep his head above water as he fought to get untangled from his hammock that he was still in.

Wading out in the water, I grabbed his hand and dragged him to the bank as he thrashed about wildly. Quickly untangling him from the canvas and rope, I helped him out of the water and up on the bank.

"I told you that thing didn't look safe!" Uncle Abe's hammock had come loose, wrapping him up like a burrito and he had rolled down the bank and into the river. His haphazardly built hammock had almost turned into his coffin.

"Are you all right?"

"Do I look all right? I almost drowned in that dang thing."

"I'll help you set it back up if you want me to," I offered.

"I ain't getting back in that death trap. I'll sleep on the ground," He proclaimed.

"What about the red bugs and snakes?" I picked at him.

"I'd rather die from a snake bite than drown and I'll just have to take my chances with the red bugs."

"Well, I hate to say I told you so, but I told you so," I laughed. Uncle Abe grunted his discontent and laid down on my bed, soaking wet.

I added some wood to the fire, rebaited the catfish poles and sat back to enjoy the night. It was a clear night with all the stars sparkling and winking at me. Occasionally, a falling star would streak across the sky, setting my mind to wondering how far away it was and where it would end up. I grinned as I thought about Uncle Abe tangled up in that hammock and fell asleep by the fire.

As the night gave up its hold to light, I was awakened by Uncle Abe building the fire back up. He had caught a chill in the night air, being soaking wet when he had gone to bed and was trying to dry out.

"You mind fixing me a cup of coffee since your up?" I asked as I sat up. Uncle Abe didn't say a word. "And some bacon and eggs would be nice, too. Since you took my bed, you ought to fix my breakfast." This brought a dim smile to his face as he thought about taking my bed.

"Let's go catch that bass and then we'll eat," he said as he rubbed his hands together and headed to the boat.

I silently paddled him around the point where old big mouth lived and he made his cast. Over and over he cast and twitched his lure, but wasn't having any luck.

After thirty minutes I told him that I didn't think she was going to bite and he said, "One more cast." Ten more minutes. "One more cast." Five more minutes. "One more cast." Finally, I started paddling back to camp. "Just one more cast," he said.

"Just one more thousand casts is more like it. This ship is going to dock. I'm hungry!" I paddled back to camp with Uncle Abe pouting the whole way.

With the smell of bacon frying in the air, Uncle Abe emerged from his sullen shell. "I can't understand why she didn't hit this morning."

"Maybe somebody caught her yesterday. If Hank Peters came anywhere close to her, he probably caught her. He's one of the best fishermen around," I riled him.

"Hank Peters couldn't catch squat. He's a perch jerker; don't know nothing about catching bass." Hank Peters and Uncle Abe had a competition going on, always trying to outdo each other. There was no love loss between them.

We ate a pound of bacon and a dozen eggs. Food just seems to taste better when it's cooked over an open fire and a person seems to eat more when they are sleeping outside under the stars.

After breakfast, Uncle Abe laid back down on my bed, which was still wet. I was a little restless and said, "Let's go chase those goats and see if we can catch one. It will be fun and we can get our exercise for today."

"Exercise? I got my exercise last night. I'm going to take a nap," said Uncle Abe as he pulled his hat down over his eyes.

"I'll just go chase goats myself," I said and set off to explore the island. I found the goats down on the far end of the island, no doubt trying to keep their distance from us. There were four nannies, six young goats and one big billy. He had a full curl of horns and smelled awful.

As I circled around them, the billy kept a close eye on me. The other goats trotted off a few feet, but he stood his ground as if daring me to come any closer. *"I'll rush him and he'll run off,"* I thought and made a mad dash at the goats. They took off and hightailed it out of there. That is, all of them except the billy. He didn't move and I was going to call his bluff. I couldn't let myself be outdone by a goat. Somebody might find out.

Almost upon him, I realized that he wasn't bluffing, but I couldn't stop quickly enough. He hit me right in the belly, knocking me flat on my back.

Boy, that hurt and as I rose up trying to catch my breath, he pranced off to join the other goats. I was just glad that he didn't stay to finish the job.

Regaining my composure and my breath, he wouldn't catch me like that again. I found a good sturdy stick and took out after them again. I was herding them back toward camp to disturb Uncle Abe's nap.

As I ran the goats across the island, I came upon an old shack made out of tin. Someone had apparently built it for the goats to have shelter from the rain. Looking inside, there was a salt block and a whole lot of goat droppings, but it was dry.

I finally herded the goats right through camp and hollered, "Stampede!" Uncle Abe was jolted from his sleep just as one of the goats ran under the tarp and jumped right over him.

A frightened, "Aaaaah!" was all that he could get out as he thought that he was under some kind of attack.

I laughed so hard that it hurt as Uncle Abe bolted out from under the tarp with his fist balled up, looking this way and that. "What are you going to do? Beat up the goats?" I laughed.

Then I had to run for my life as Uncle Abe was charging me like a bull after red. All I can say is it's a good thing that I was faster than him. There's no telling what he would have done to me if he had caught me.

After two laps around the island, he gave out of breath and sat down on a stump. I laid low for the rest of the day to give him time to cool off and didn't return to camp until just before dark.

Slipping back into camp while Uncle Abe was frying some fish, I said, "That fish sure smells good," and it did. All I had found to eat since breakfast was a few muscadines and I was hungry, but I didn't expect him to offer me any.

"Come on and get you some. I know you must be hungry," he offered in a friendly voice.

"You're not mad at me?" I asked.

"Naw, after I cooled off, I laughed about it. I've never been in a goat stampede before."

I came on in and got a plate of fish and sat down to eat. Uncle Abe was grinning.

"Every dog has his day. You had yours and I'll have mine," he said, looking at me with a smirk on his face.

Uncle Abe took my bed again that night, while I slept on the ground by the fire. I waited until I heard him snoring before I let myself fall asleep, knowing that I had to watch him. He would get even.

Morning came after a long night of rolling around on the ground trying to get comfortable. I didn't sleep much that night between lying on the hard ground and keeping an eye out for Uncle Abe.

Uncle Abe made coffee and handed me a cup. He was being much too nice. I wondered what fate he was contriving for me. We drank our coffee with pleasant conversation and got in the boat for our morning round.

I paddled around the point as usual. Uncle Abe cast as usual and the bass didn't bite, just like the day before. Uncle Abe decided she had probably caught on to his lure, so I paddled us back to camp.

We had another good breakfast and I set out to gather material for another bed while Uncle Abe was busy tinkering with his lure. I ran into the goats about halfway of the island, guessing that they were getting used to us and had moved a little closer each day.

The billy kept an eye on me and I kept an eye on him, not wanting to tangle with him today. He was a mean old goat and I decided to give him a name. Just any old name wouldn't do; it had to be fitting to his demeanor, which was downright meanness.

"I'll call you Krushchev," I told him, as he looked at me with uncaring eyes. The name didn't seem to faze him, so I went on with my business.

I finished the bed and had to stand back and smile as I admired my handiwork. It was a much finer bed than the first one. Maybe I would get some sleep tonight.

"Finished!" Uncle Abe exclaimed as he held up his born again lure. I examined it and found that he had carved little grooves down each side to make it sound different in the water, then taken polk salad berries and stained it a reddish–purple color. Finishing it off with a piece of charred wood, he colored the grooves black and drew a smile on its face.

"Uncle Abe, you've outdone yourself this time. If she won't bite this lure, she ain't there, but what's the smile for?"

"Well, if she's not hungry, the smile will make her mad and she'll bite anyway," he smiled as he looked at the lure, admiring his creation.

"Let's go try it out!" I said excitedly. "I've got to see that baby in action."

"We'll have to wait until tomorrow. Give it time to dry. You can't rush perfection," he said with dignity.

We ate beans and bread that night, being so busy with the bed and the lure that we had forgotten to catch some catfish. Uncle Abe took my new bed. At least I wouldn't have to sleep on the hard ground tonight. I settled for the old bed.

I was awakened to the hollering of Uncle Abe. "It's got me! Randy, come here quick!" and there was splashing in the river.

Not knowing what was going on, I jumped out of bed and took off running and fell flat on my face. I hit the ground so hard that it almost knocked me out, but Uncle Abe's laughter brought me back from the dark.

"You all right, boy? Let me help you up," he laughed. I shook my head to clear it and started to get up, but something had me. Looking down at my feet I could see the rope tied around my ankle. Sometime during the night, Uncle Abe had set his trap and I had run right into it.

I sat up moaning, looked at Uncle Abe who was scratching and laughing at the same time.

"Are we square now?" I painfully asked.

"Square," he said and started scratching and fetching like something was eating him alive. "Dad–blame redbugs," he swore. "Let's go fishing."

As I was paddling him around the point, we saw another boat coming in on the other side. It was Hank Peters and he was headed for Uncle

Abe's big bass. Uncle Abe was scratching his red-bugs and snarling at Hank Peters at the same time.

"Paddle faster," he said and I blocked Hank Peters from the log.

"Move out of the way Abe. I'm fishing that log," demanded Peters.

"No, you ain't and you might as well paddle back to where you come from," Uncle Abe stated. These were two hard headed old men.

"I aim to fish that log and if I have to run over you to do it, so be it."

"I don't think so Peters." Uncle Abe reached in his back pocket and pulled out his slingshot. He carried his ammunition in his overall bib pocket and pulled out a small round rock.

"You ain't going to do nothing with that," Peters said with some uncertainty in his voice.

"Start paddling Peters," Uncle Abe said as he raised his slingshot.

"Hmm! I ain't...." he started as the rock hit him right in the chest.

"Dang–it Abe! That hurt."

"Start paddling," Uncle Abe demanded as he fired another shot that hit Peters in the arm. I guess the last shot convinced Peters, because he put it in high gear. Fast as I ever saw a man paddle.

Uncle Abe sat there glowing with victory and scratching. "You'll pay for this Abe!" Peters shouted and waived his fist in the air. Uncle Abe reached for another rock.

"You can't hit him from here. He's three or four hundred feet away," I told him, but he took aim anyway. He tested the wind and elevated his shot like an artillery specialist. Releasing his shot, the rock sailed through the air on a big arch, hitting Peters smack in the back of the head. I just thought he was paddling fast before. Now he had it in overdrive.

Uncle Abe jumped up in the boat doing a jig, scratching and celebrating. He jumped up on the seat, hollering and waving his slingshot in the air. "Come on back if you ever want some more!" He kicked at Peters while he was down.

I probably shouldn't have done it, but I just couldn't resist. He was dancing around on the boat seat like a teenager and he did need a bath. I pulled the front of the boat around with one swift stroke of my paddle, dumping Uncle Abe right in the river.

Luckily, he didn't even get mad, being so overjoyed that he had put Peters down the road. He was holding onto the boat with one hand, waving his slingshot with the other and singing some kind of Indian victory song while his hat floated off down the river.

I helped him into the boat and we paddled back to camp. There had been too much disturbance to try and catch the bass this morning.

Uncle Abe jumped out of the boat in the best mood that I'd seen him, in years. Even with the redbugs eating him alive, he was still pleasant.

He started pulling off his clothes and hanging them on the tree limbs to dry. "How about getting me a couple of handfuls of that red clay from the river bank?" he said as he stripped butt naked.

I returned with the red clay and noticed the whelps all over his body as he clawed at them. "What are you going to do with the clay?" I asked.

"I'm going to smother the little buggers," he said as I handed him the clay.

"Well, I had better get some more if you're going to smother all of them."

He covered his whole body except his face with that clay. I suppose redbugs don't like your face? He looked like–like I don't know what he looked like, but at least I convinced him to put his boxers back on.

I spent the rest of the day catching catfish and preparing supper. Uncle Abe was in no shape to lend a hand. He just laid around dressed in mud. Actually, I think it must have helped because he wasn't scratching near as much.

We had a good supper consisting of catfish, taters & onions, beans and bread, then turned in early. It had been a very eventful day and we were tired. I looked over at Uncle Abe on his new bed and saw him smiling as I drifted off to sleep.

Cla–Boom! The ground shook and lightning flashed, scaring us half to death. We both sat up and were wide awake. Rain started coming down and the wind ripped our tarp right out from over us.

"Tornado!" Uncle Abe shouted, over the roar of the wind. I don't know whether it was a tornado or not, but we were in one bad storm. "We've got to find shelter!" he hollered and took off running blindly through the woods. Finally,

I caught up to him and grabbing his arm, asked him, "Where are you going?"

"I don't know," he said out of breath and bleeding from the briers and bushes that he had just run through.

"Come on. There's a shed that somebody built for the goats. If it didn't blow away, we can get out of the rain."

I led the way to the goat shed through the pitch black night, catching glimpses of where I was going when the lightning flashed. The wind had died down, but it was raining cats and dogs by the time we finally found the shed.

"Over here!" I called and ducked down to go into the shed. The next thing I knew, I was laying flat on my back in the pouring rain. Old Krushchev had met me at the door and let me know that I wasn't welcome in his house.

Uncle Abe helped me up and we stood there shivering and wondering what to do next. I could see Uncle Abe when the lightning flashed. All he had on was his boxers. Most of the clay had been washed off by the rain, exposing the whelps and scratches all over his body.

After twenty minutes of standing in the soaking rain, Uncle Abe had had about all he could stand. "I'm going in!" he shouted and Krushchev met him at the door. The goat hit him hard, but Uncle Abe was at the end of his rope. He was not going to be denied by a goat.

There was an awful fight as Krushchev and Uncle Abe butted heads. Uncle Abe had a hold of Krushchev's horns and they were going round and round in that shed with the other goats darting out into the rain and then back in again. Goats don't like to get wet.

Uncle Abe put a spin move on Krushchev and got him in a headlock, throwing him to the ground and subduing him.

"All clear!" he hollered and I came in out of the rain.

As bad as it smelled, I was glad to be in the dry and squatted down in the middle of the goats. Uncle Abe had found his spot, using Krushchev for a backrest with his arm still around the goat to hold him down.

The rain continued until the early morning hours as I nodded in and out of sleep. Then it stopped raining just after daylight. Time to get out of here and into some fresh air.

I could hear Uncle Abe snoring and looked over at him laying in a pile of goat droppings and using Krushchev for a pillow. I would have given anything for a camera to capture the moment right then and could have held Uncle Abe over a barrel for the rest of his life.

Getting some fresh air outside, I banged on the side of the shed and Uncle Abe came crawling out on his hands and knees. Then he shot forward, flat on his face in the mud as Krushchev butted him right on his boxer covered behind and curled his lip up in a jester which I took as, "Take that."

I felt sorry for Uncle Abe as I helped him to his feet. He was cold, almost naked, scratched up, half eaten up by redbugs, stiff and sore from our night in the goat shed and just downright miserable looking.

He looked at me with eyes that looked somewhere between begging for relief and being ready to take on anything else that might happen. "I'm going home," he said. Knowing that he meant what he said, I refrained from commenting and followed him back to camp or what was left of camp.

The storm had really done a number on our home away from home. The beds that I had made were totally gone, a tree blown down across where they had laid. Uncle Abe's clothes were nowhere to be found. Only his boots remained and he quickly put them on his sore feet, as if he were afraid something would happen to them, too.

The only bright spot was that the boat was still there, although it was blown halfway up on the bank and the paddles and fishing poles were still intact. Thank goodness for that. At least we wouldn't have to swim home.

Uncle Abe, with his boots on, looked around at the mess and said, "Let's go," as he headed for the boat. Shoving off, we left camp zero and didn't look back.

As we came around the point of the island, I was wondering if Uncle Abe was even thinking about that bass. I didn't have to wonder long, as he reached for his pole and said, "Hold on."

After all that he had been through, I must say that it didn't effect his casting ability, for he laid his newly altered lure, that he hadn't even had a chance to use, right beside the log.

With his full attention on his lure, he twitched it three times and then twice. I don't know whether it was the twitching or the smile that he had drawn on the lure's face, but it worked. That bass tore into it with a vengeance.

I backed the boat out to deeper water as Uncle Abe held on with all he had. The bass stripping drag at will and then leaping out of the water, shaking her head, trying to remove the lure that was stuck in her face.

The lure held as the bass put up a magnificent battle and Uncle Abe was determined to win this one. Pulling the bass to the right and then to the left, he slowly wore her down. She made one last jump and turned up on her side all tuckered out. Uncle Abe reached down and grabbed her lower lip and lifted her into the boat.

I let out a whoop! He had finally caught her, after all these years and all the lures that she had broke off. He held her up and looked at her, she was one massive bass. Just guessing, I would say thirteen pounds.

Uncle Abe removed the lure and kissed the bass on top of the head with the utmost respect. Then to my amazement, he laid her gently back in the water and watched her swim away with a thin, tight lipped smile on his face.

"After all these years, you finally caught her. Then you turn her loose. What's gotten into you?" I scolded him.

"I'm not ready for it to be over just yet," he said staring into the water. "If I was to keep her, I'd have no reason to come back and I need that reason to keep me going. Now let's go. I've got to go face your Aunt Lilly."

I paddled and thought about Uncle Abe releasing that bass and had to admire him. He was a true sportsman and probably the only man alive that had caught and released a thirteen pound bass, while wearing nothing but boxers and boots. I couldn't help but laugh out loud. Uncle Abe grunted and kept on paddling.

We pulled up to the landing, removed our gear, which wasn't much thanks to the storm that had consumed most of it and I walked Uncle Abe to his house. I really wouldn't feel right letting a man in his condition and attire go it on his own. If anyone saw him, they would think that he had lost his mind.

Uncle Abe knew that he would be in hot water for slipping off on this camping trip, but he had a plan. Outdoorsman can always seem to come up with a good story or excuse. He would play on Aunt Lilly's sympathetic side and she would be so caught up by the condition of his scratched, bitten, bruised, naked, aching and smelly body that she wouldn't come down on him so hard.

Uncle Abe walked up on the porch and I stayed in the yard to avoid any shrapnel that might be flying around. He knocked on the door and stood there with the most pitiful face that you've ever seen.

I heard Aunt Lilly gasp as she saw him. "Abe! What in the world happened to you? Are you alright?" Uncle Abe didn't say a word, but staggered a little and Aunt Lilly caught him. "What happened, honey?" He put on a good show as he struggled to respond.

"Tornado!"

Aunt Lilly glanced over at me and I confirmed, "We got caught in a bad storm last night. Lucky to be alive!" I added.

"Come on Abe, let's get you inside and get you doctored up," she said as she wrapped an arm around him to help him in.

As they went through the door, Uncle Abe turned his head toward me and winked. I could hear Aunt Lilly as she helped him in. "Lord, Abe, you smell like a billy goat. Didn't you take a bath while you were gone? What happened to your clothes?"

I heard Uncle Abe one more time "Tornado!" with a more distressed voice and then something about a bath tub from Aunt Lilly. Uncle Abe was pretty slick, but I couldn't believe that he had fooled Aunt Lilly that easily.

I was smiling as I walked down the road, thinking about how Uncle Abe had pulled that off. Then I heard him screaming as Aunt Lilly bathed him down with alcohol. Quickening my pace, I headed home.

The moral of this story is…
You may be slick, but you can't slide on barbwire.

Epilogue: The Truth

The true story of my life is actually not very far off from the stories that you've just read. My Great Grandparents, Grandparents, and parents lived along the banks of the Coosa River in central Alabama and I have spent most of my life watching sunrises across the waters of the Coosa. "There comes Big Red," was the term we often used as the sun came up over the far mountains with its reddish–orange, early morning hue.

After bringing five boys into the world, Paw and Maw finally had a girl and decided that their clan was big enough. With help from Grandparents, Aunts, and Uncles, they managed to raise us in a way that we will never forget. There is a great deal of respect for Paw and Maw from all of their children, and rightly so, because they earned it.

We spent a lot of time fishing and hunting which was a good thing because we learned about the great outdoors and helped put food on the table also. Much of the rest of our time was spent in the garden and tending animals. We had pigs, goats, chickens and an occasional cow to milk.

One of my jobs was to milk the goat. Yes, we drank goat milk and my younger brothers would occasionally get it hot, right out of the goat. Of course, I encouraged this and since I was the chief goat milker, I could give an occasional squirt to an open mouth.

We spent a lot of time in the woods and the river. There was no time for boredom. If there wasn't something to do, we created something. Being fortunate enough to live on the river led to many exciting adventures. It also provided an income for someone willing to put a little elbow grease into it. I made my gas and spending money by selling catfish and the elbow grease came in when you caught enough bait for six hundred trot line hooks, two times a day. Very hard work, yes, but very rewarding.

As far as the stories that I wrote about, yes we caught giant catfish, got chased by a U.F.O, followed trails through Brandy Holler, talked to the owls, caught turtles, sat on the porch and listened to the old–timers tell their stories, caught snakes, played on Gold Hill, chased beavers, went to church, trapped fur–bearers, sold catfish, went possum and coon hunting, had some of the best hunting dogs there were, camped on Goat Island, had a mean goat named Krushchev and generally had the best childhood that anyone could ask for. Although the stories were stretched a tad, there is a lot of truth in them and they were a whole lot of fun.

I still remember the first cottonmouth that I caught and the trouble that I got into when I proudly carried it into the house wrapped, around my arm. Maw wasn't real happy with me that day! We also had some very strange things happen. Like the time that my older brother and I were waterskiing. We had a competition going on to see who could ski onto the bank and jump out of their skis without getting our feet wet. Well, he skied up onto the bank and there happened to be a fire there and he happened to fall right into the fire. I'll never forget how fast that he got back up and into the water.

One day, when I was probably ten years old, we heard a big bullfrog croaking in the boathouse. Paw told me to stand by a hole in the side of the boathouse and that he would go in there and run that frog out.

"When he comes out of that hole, don't let him get by you." He told me, and I thought that I was ready, but that frog went right between my legs. I remember the dark gloom that came over me as I was thinking that I had failed Paw and that was the last thing in the world that I wanted to do. The frog made two hops and sailed off a three foot bank and into the river. In desperation, not wanting to let Paw down, I sailed off the bank right behind that frog. It seemed as though I sailed through the air in slow motion for the longest time and there was panic going through my young mind as the frog hit the water ahead of me. To my amazement, I came down in the water right on top of that big frog, grabbing him with both hands. As I was coming out of the water, Paw came around the boathouse and was grinning from ear to ear when he saw me holding that frog. It's memories of moments like that I will always cherish. For a young boy, seeing that I had pleased Paw was the ultimate goal, it just didn't get any better than that.

After a few broken bones and an unknown number of stitches, we managed to grow up. The lessons that we learned stuck with us and we passed them on to our children. Now, I find myself passing them on to my grandchildren with hopes that they will enjoy them as much as I did.

As I finish my writings, I smile and reminisce about the "Good Old Days" as Paw called them. Just before he passed away, on his last trip to the hospital, he looked around at everything as we drove off. He wasn't saying anything, just looking. When I asked him, "Paw, what are you thinking about?"

He said, "Just thinking about the 'Good Old Days.'"

Paw never made it back down to the river. He passed away later that week in the hospital, but he left his legacy with all of his children, grandchildren, and great–grandchildren. We'll cherish and remember the "Good Old Days" with Paw, but we'll carry on because of him and there will be some more "Good Old Days." I am sure of it!

The moral of this book is…
Fond memories always with us.
Reminiscing days gone by.
Regret and suffering, contrariwise.
Look to the future with open eyes.

Life on the River continues 2008